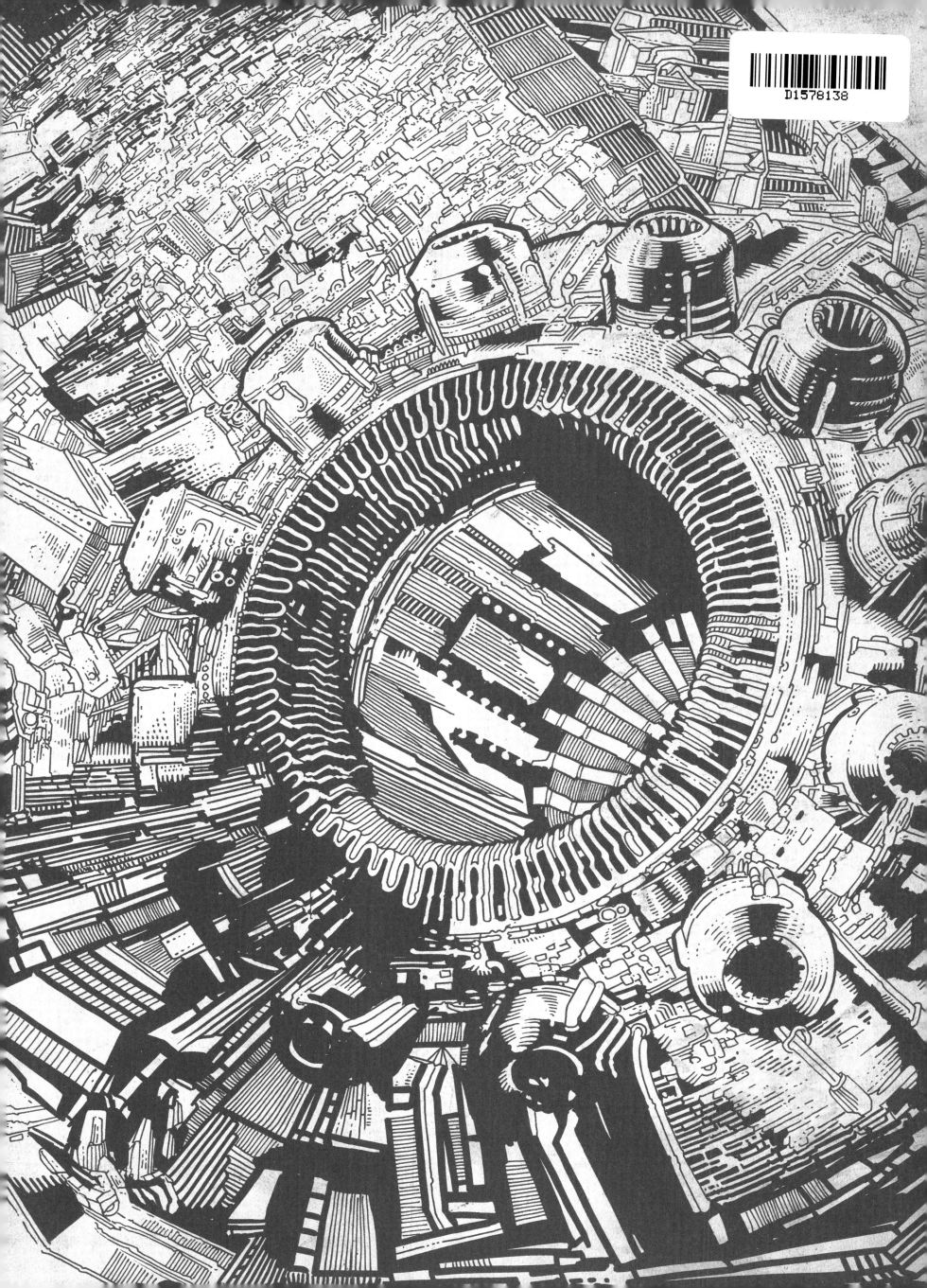

STAR WARS

GALACTIC ATLAS

EGMONT
We bring stories to life

First published in Great Britain 2016
by Egmont UK Limited, The Yellow Building,
1 Nicholas Road, London W11 4AN

Illustrated by Tim McDonagh
Written and edited by Emil Fortune
Designed by Richie Hull

Many thanks to Michael Siglain, Samantha Holland,
Pablo Hidalgo, Jason Fry, Matt Martin and everyone else
who helped put this book together.

© & ™ 2016 Lucasfilm Ltd.

ISBN 978 1 4052 7998 7
62478/9

Printed in Poland

To find more great *Star Wars* books, visit
www.egmont.co.uk/starwars

STAR WARS

GALACTIC ATLAS

ILLUSTRATED BY
TIM McDONAGH

INTRODUCTION

The Graf Archive covers the majority of the moon Orchis 2; its endless shelves, galleries and databanks contain texts, artworks, antiques, and even preserved plants and animals from every part of the galaxy.

Many items which cannot immediately be identified are moved to the underground Shadow Stacks, where they wait to be processed, often for many years. Venturing into these dusty basements is an important part of an Archivist's training, a kind of final exam: the challenge is to come back with a unexpected treasure. It can even be dangerous, as one young student discovered when the mummified ghest he was examining turned out to be merely hibernating…

These ancient hand-drawn maps were unearthed from the Shadow Stacks by a far luckier student. The Head Curator's theory is that they are the work of the great Ithorian artist Gammit Chond. We know only a little about Chond – few of his works have survived – but these maps show much of his characteristic style and flair.

Chond never travelled offworld, and one history has it that he never ventured more than a day's walk from his home. He was, however, fascinated by travellers' tales, and many of his works depict their stories of adventure and discovery in the rest of the galaxy.

They are not, of course, strictly accurate. You would not be advised to try to cross the Jundland Wastes using Chond's map of Tatooine. The artist was more interested in the feel of these strange worlds, and the often galaxy-shaking events which took place on them.

Taken together, they seem to be centred on the saga of the legendary Skywalker family. While we know that many of the things he has included are a matter of fact, some may merely be tall tales spun by explorers; but it all presents a unique view of a fascinating slice of history.

After several years of painstaking restoration, it is my great privilege, and that of the Graf Archive, to present this never-before-seen trove of art to the galaxy.

— Amel Fortoon,
Director, Graf Archive

THE GALAXY

The galaxy is generally thought to be divided into the following regions. Galactic North is the direction towards the top of this chart.

Deep Core: Densely packed stars rotate around the super-massive black hole at the heart of the galaxy. It is dangerous to navigate, and few travellers venture this far coreward.

Core Worlds: The richest and most important worlds cluster around the edges of the Deep Core. These include Coruscant, Corellia, Kuat, Hosnian Prime and other key systems.

Colonies: This region contains planets colonised by the Core Worlds. The Colonies sit along major trade routes and some of them are extremely wealthy.

Inner Rim: When first settled, this area was known simply as 'the Rim' – it was the frontier of galactic civilisation for centuries. As colonisation spread outwards, the Inner Rim worlds prospered.

Expansion Region: With competition for resources comes the need to expand, and the Expansion Region contains newer colonies sponsored by their coreward neighbours.

Mid Rim: Many important worlds are found in the Mid Rim, including Naboo, Kashyyyk, Ithor and Malastare. Because it is relatively far from the Core, travellers should be wary of pirates.

Outer Rim Territories: The largest region of the known galaxy is the Outer Rim, which contains many strange and often savage worlds. Some of the most important worlds in the Confederacy of Independent Systems – otherwise known as the Separatists, during the Clone Wars – were in this region.

Unknown Regions: The Westward arm of the galaxy is mapped but largely unexplored. Who knows what lurks in the dark spaces beyond the frontiers of galactic civilisation?

Wild Space: Beyond the Outer Rim lies the unmapped expanse of Wild Space. Explorers and cartographers seek their fortune here at their peril.

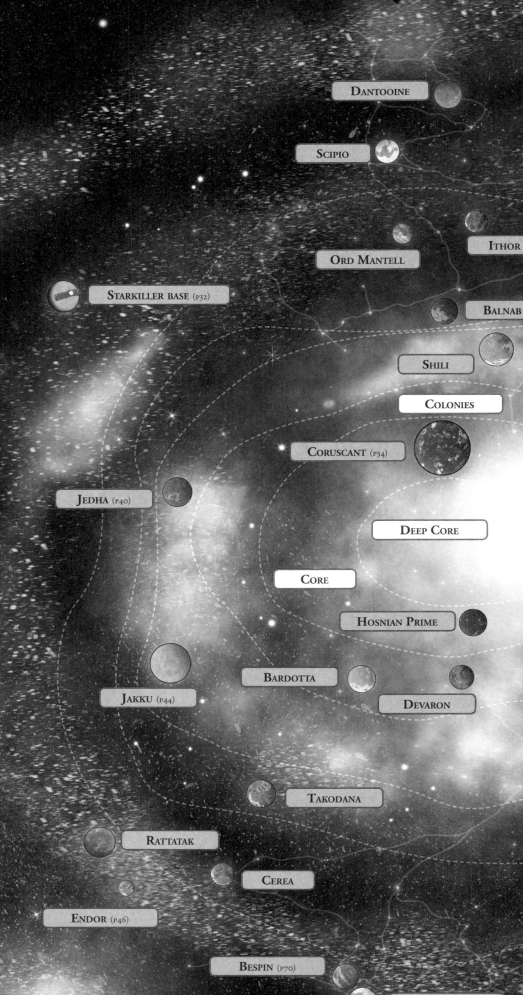

MORTIS (p26)

DANTOOINE

SCIPIO

ITHOR

ORD MANTELL

BALNAB

STARKILLER BASE (p32)

SHILI

COLONIES

CORUSCANT (p34)

JEDHA (p40)

DEEP CORE

CORE

HOSNIAN PRIME

BARDOTTA

JAKKU (p44)

DEVARON

TAKODANA

RATTATAK

CEREA

ENDOR (p46)

BESPIN (p70)

HOTH (p62)

MUSTAFAR (p74)

POLIS MASSA

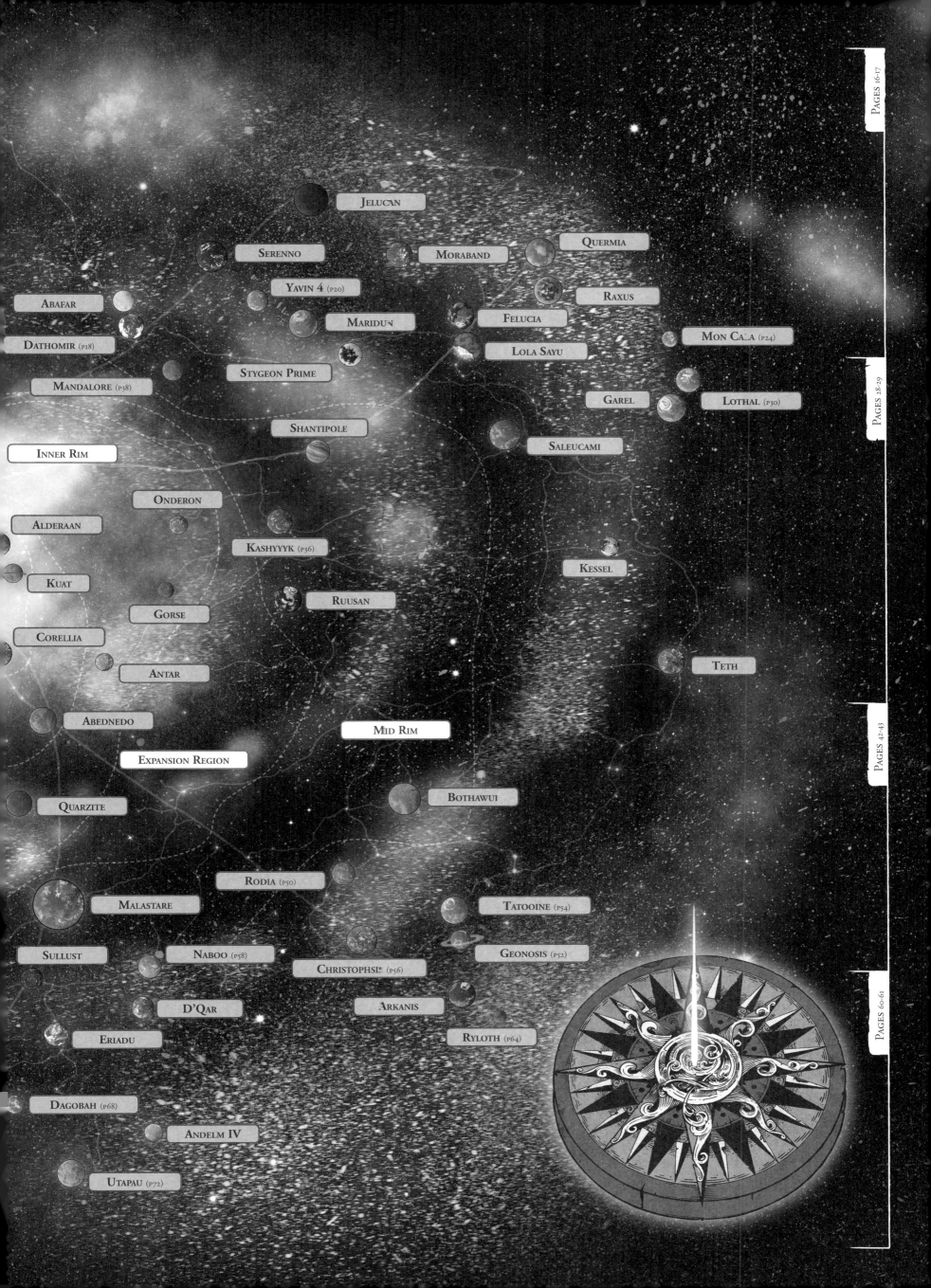

JELUCAN

SERENNO

MORABAND

QUERMIA

RAXUS

ABAFAR

YAVIN 4 (P20)

MARIDUN

FELUCIA

MON CALA (P24)

DATHOMIR (P18)

LOLA SAYU

MANDALORE (P38)

STYGEON PRIME

GAREL

LOTHAL (P30)

SHANTIPOLE

INNER RIM

SALEUCAMI

ONDERON

ALDERAAN

KASHYYYK (P36)

KESSEL

KUAT

RUUSAN

GORSE

CORELLIA

TETH

ANTAR

ABEDNEDO

MID RIM

EXPANSION REGION

QUARZITE

BOTHAWUI

RODIA (P50)

MALASTARE

TATOOINE (P54)

SULLUST

NABOO (P58)

GEONOSIS (P52)

CHRISTOPHSIS (P56)

D'QAR

ARKANIS

ERIADU

RYLOTH (P64)

DAGOBAH (P68)

ANDELM IV

UTAPAU (P72)

PAGES 16-17

PAGES 28-29

PAGES 42-43

PAGES 60-61

Timeline

This timeline describes the period of history covered in these maps, from the Clone Wars between the Republic and the Separatists, to the Galactic Civil War between the Empire and the Rebel Alliance, and beyond.
Dates in this book are given using the 'ABY-BBY' dating system, which is centred around the Battle of Yavin, when the first Death Star was destroyed. Therefore, 5 BBY is five years before the Battle of Yavin, and 5 ABY is five years after.

32 BBY The galaxy is governed by the Republic. On Coruscant, the capital world, Senators from a thousand worlds meet to debate the future, while the Jedi Order maintains peace and harmony.

The powerful Trade Federation, which controls galactic trade, bullies the remote world Naboo. Two Jedi, Qui-Gon Jinn and Obi-Wan Kenobi, are sent to negotiate peace. However, the Trade Federation tries to assassinate the Jedi and sends their battle droid armies down to the planet to capture Queen Padmé Amidala.

Qui-Gon Jinn and Obi-Wan Kenobi rescue the Queen, but are forced to flee. Their ship needs repairs, so they stop on the remote desert world Tatooine. Here they meet the slave boy Anakin Skywalker, whose potential as a Jedi is the greatest Qui-Gon has ever seen. The Jedi win Anakin's freedom and take him away with them.

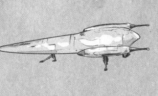

The Jedi escort Queen Amidala to Coruscant, but she cannot persuade the Senate to help Naboo. She returns to her homeworld with Qui-Gon, Obi-Wan and Anakin, and their Gungan friend Jar Jar Binks. The Gungans fight a battle against the Trade Federation's droid army as the Queen retakes her palace.

A sinister and deadly assassin has been tracking the Jedi: the Sith Lord Darth Maul. He and his Master, Darth Sidious, are secretly behind the Trade Federation's invasion. In a fierce battle beneath the city of Theed, he slays Qui-Gon Jinn, but is himself cut in half by Obi-Wan and seemingly destroyed.

32 BBY The Gungans and the Naboo defeat the droid army with the help of Anakin Skywalker. The Trade Federation is forced to withdraw.

22 BBY Senator Palpatine of Naboo has been made Supreme Chancellor. Secretly, he is the evil Sith Lord Darth Sidious. He plans to start a galactic war to scare the Republic into building up the military he needs in order to seize absolute power for himself.

The former Jedi Master Count Dooku has sparked a crisis, with his Confederacy of Independent Systems – the so-called Separatists – threatening to split from the Republic. The Senate must decide whether or not to create an Army of the Republic. One prominent opponent of this plan is Padmé Amidala, who is now a Senator.

A series of attempts on Senator Amidala's life leads Obi-Wan Kenobi to the planet Kamino. Here he discovers an army of clones, secretly ordered by a now-dead Jedi Master, and based on the bounty hunter Jango Fett, who is the assassin he has been seeking. He follows Fett to Geonosis.

Anakin, now a Jedi apprentice, is assigned to protect Padmé. They travel to Naboo, where they begin to fall in love. Anakin is troubled by dreams about his mother, Shmi, whom he was forced to leave behind on Tatooine many years ago.

On Tatooine, Anakin discovers that his mother has been kidnapped by the Sand People. He is unable to save her life, and in a rage, he slaughters the tribe.

Obi-Wan is captured on Geonosis by the Separatists, as are Anakin and Padmé when they try to rescue him.

Jedi Master Mace Windu leads a team of Jedi to the rescue, backed by the clone army that now serves the Republic. Windu slays Fett, but Count Dooku escapes, pursued by Anakin Skywalker and Obi-Wan Kenobi.

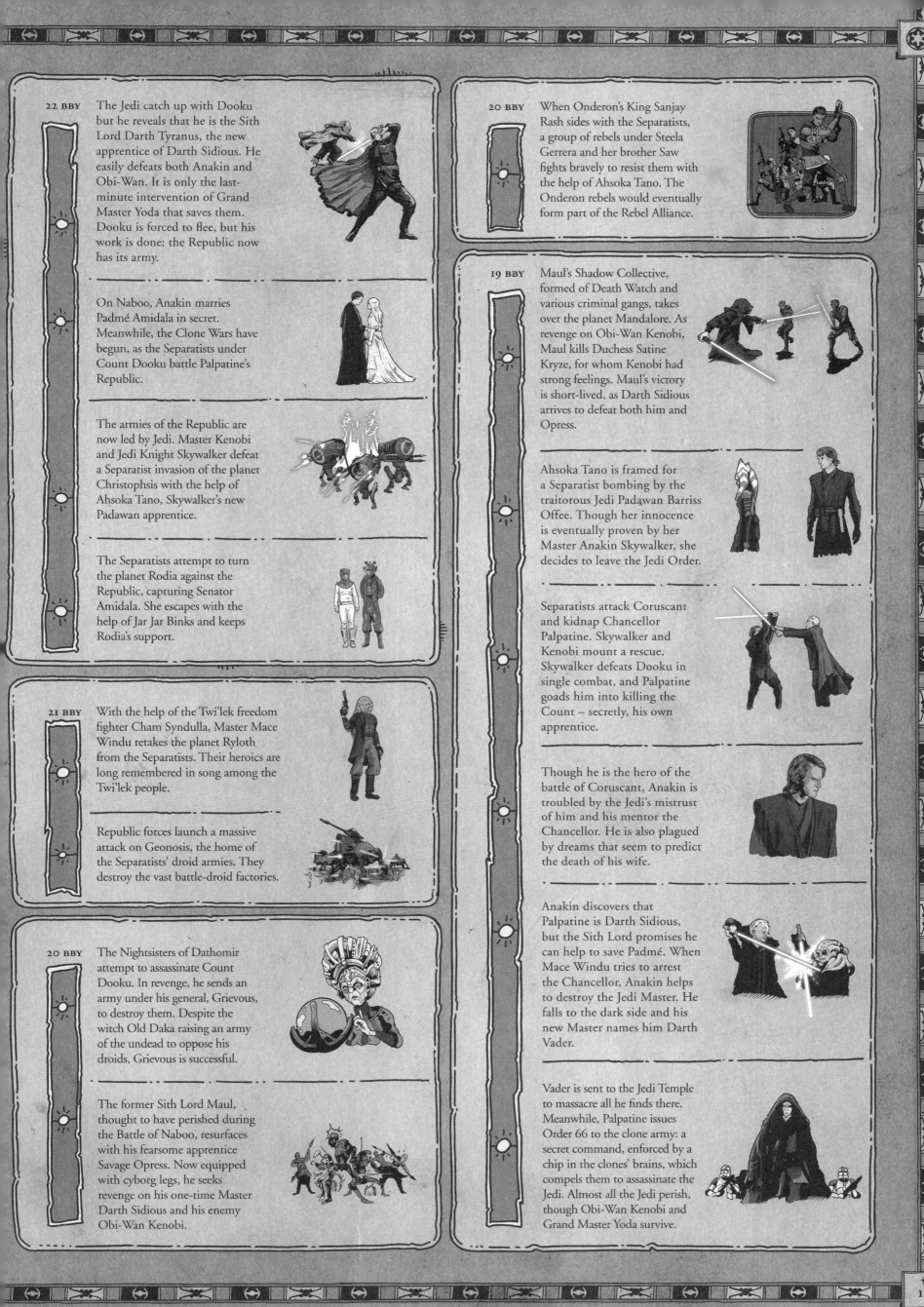

22 BBY

The Jedi catch up with Dooku but he reveals that he is the Sith Lord Darth Tyranus, the new apprentice of Darth Sidious. He easily defeats both Anakin and Obi-Wan. It is only the last-minute intervention of Grand Master Yoda that saves them. Dooku is forced to flee, but his work is done: the Republic now has its army.

On Naboo, Anakin marries Padmé Amidala in secret. Meanwhile, the Clone Wars have begun, as the Separatists under Count Dooku battle Palpatine's Republic.

The armies of the Republic are now led by Jedi. Master Kenobi and Jedi Knight Skywalker defeat a Separatist invasion of the planet Christophsis with the help of Ahsoka Tano, Skywalker's new Padawan apprentice.

The Separatists attempt to turn the planet Rodia against the Republic, capturing Senator Amidala. She escapes with the help of Jar Jar Binks and keeps Rodia's support.

21 BBY

With the help of the Twi'lek freedom fighter Cham Syndulla, Master Mace Windu retakes the planet Ryloth from the Separatists. Their heroics are long remembered in song among the Twi'lek people.

Republic forces launch a massive attack on Geonosis, the home of the Separatists' droid armies. They destroy the vast battle-droid factories.

20 BBY

The Nightsisters of Dathomir attempt to assassinate Count Dooku. In revenge, he sends an army under his general, Grievous, to destroy them. Despite the witch Old Daka raising an army of the undead to oppose his droids, Grievous is successful.

The former Sith Lord Maul, thought to have perished during the Battle of Naboo, resurfaces with his fearsome apprentice Savage Opress. Now equipped with cyborg legs, he seeks revenge on his one-time Master Darth Sidious and his enemy Obi-Wan Kenobi.

20 BBY

When Onderon's King Sanjay Rash sides with the Separatists, a group of rebels under Steela Gerrera and her brother Saw fights bravely to resist them with the help of Ahsoka Tano. The Onderon rebels would eventually form part of the Rebel Alliance.

19 BBY

Maul's Shadow Collective, formed of Death Watch and various criminal gangs, takes over the planet Mandalore. As revenge on Obi-Wan Kenobi, Maul kills Duchess Satine Kryze, for whom Kenobi had strong feelings. Maul's victory is short-lived, as Darth Sidious arrives to defeat both him and Opress.

Ahsoka Tano is framed for a Separatist bombing by the traitorous Jedi Padawan Barriss Offee. Though her innocence is eventually proven by her Master Anakin Skywalker, she decides to leave the Jedi Order.

Separatists attack Coruscant and kidnap Chancellor Palpatine. Skywalker and Kenobi mount a rescue. Skywalker defeats Dooku in single combat, and Palpatine goads him into killing the Count – secretly, his own apprentice.

Though he is the hero of the battle of Coruscant, Anakin is troubled by the Jedi's mistrust of him and his mentor the Chancellor. He is also plagued by dreams that seem to predict the death of his wife.

Anakin discovers that Palpatine is Darth Sidious, but the Sith Lord promises he can help to save Padmé. When Mace Windu tries to arrest the Chancellor, Anakin helps to destroy the Jedi Master. He falls to the dark side and his new Master names him Darth Vader.

Vader is sent to the Jedi Temple to massacre all he finds there. Meanwhile, Palpatine issues Order 66 to the clone army: a secret command, enforced by a chip in the clones' brains, which compels them to assassinate the Jedi. Almost all the Jedi perish, though Obi-Wan Kenobi and Grand Master Yoda survive.

19 BBY On Utapau, Obi-Wan Kenobi's clone troops have cornered General Grievous, but they turn their fire on Kenobi as Order 66 is issued. Kenobi escapes and duels Grievous, killing the cyborg.

Grand Master Yoda goes to the Senate on Coruscant to confront Darth Sidious, but he is unable to defeat the Sith Lord in combat. The Jedi retreats and exiles himself to the planet Dagobah.

Vader travels to the lava world Mustafar, where he slays the Separatist leaders, ending the Clone Wars for his Master. Obi-Wan follows him and, in an epic duel, defeats him. Vader's injuries are severe and require him to wear a cyborg suit of armour to survive from this point on.

Padmé Amidala gives birth to twins, Luke and Leia, but does not herself survive. Luke is hidden on Tatooine with the Lars family, and Leia is adopted by Senator Bail Organa of Alderaan.

Supreme Chancellor Palpatine declares himself Galactic Emperor.

5 BBY On the remote planet Lothal a group of rebels led by Hera Syndulla of Ryloth and the former Jedi Padawan Kanan Jarrus is formed. Ezra Bridger, an orphaned street thief, joins the crew of their ship the *Ghost* and begins to train in the ways of the Jedi.

4 BBY After many battles, Kanan Jarrus is captured by the Grand Inquisitor, a fearsome Jedi hunter, and taken aboard Grand Moff Tarkin's flagship the *Sovereign* in orbit above Mustafar. A daring raid by his friends frees Jarrus, who then defeats the Inquisitor in combat. The Inquisitor and the *Sovereign* are both destroyed.

0 BBY A covert team of rebel agents is tasked with a crucial mission: to steal the plans of the Empire's new battle station, the Death Star. The mission is led by Cassian Andor and Jyn Erso, and takes the Rogue One team to the planet Jedha.

0 BBY Darth Vader captures the *Tantive IV* and its passenger Princess Leia Organa, the Senator from Alderaan. He accuses her of being a rebel traitor who is in possession of the Death Star plans – but the Princess has already sent them off the ship, in the possession of her droid R2-D2.

R2-D2 and his counterpart C-3PO meet Luke Skywalker on Tatooine and take him to meet Obi-Wan Kenobi. When the Empire kills his uncle and aunt, Luke decides to train as a Jedi and to fight for the rebels against the oppressors.

Luke, Obi-Wan, R2-D2 and C-3PO travel to Mos Eisley spaceport where they hire Han Solo and Chewbacca to take them and the secret plans to the rebels on Alderaan. They travel in Solo's ship the *Millennium Falcon* to Alderaan, only to discover that the planet has been destroyed by the Death Star. The crew rescues Leia from Imperial custody and they flee to the *Millennium Falcon*.

Obi-Wan confronts his former pupil Darth Vader. He sacrifices himself, becoming one with the Force, as his friends make their escape. The Empire tracks the *Falcon* to Yavin 4.

As the Death Star closes on the rebel base, a desperate starfighter raid is launched against the battle station. Using the Force, Luke Skywalker fires the shot that destroys it, striking a key blow for the rebellion.

3 ABY Darth Vader sends probe droids across the galaxy and eventually locates the new rebel base on Hoth. His invasion force is able to destroy it, but not before the rebels escape. Meanwhile, Luke is visited by the spirit of Obi-Wan Kenobi, who tells him to travel to Dagobah.

Luke meets Yoda on Dagobah and begins his Jedi training. Han, Leia, Chewbacca and the droids stop at Bespin to repair the *Falcon*, unaware that Vader's bounty hunter Boba Fett has tracked them there.

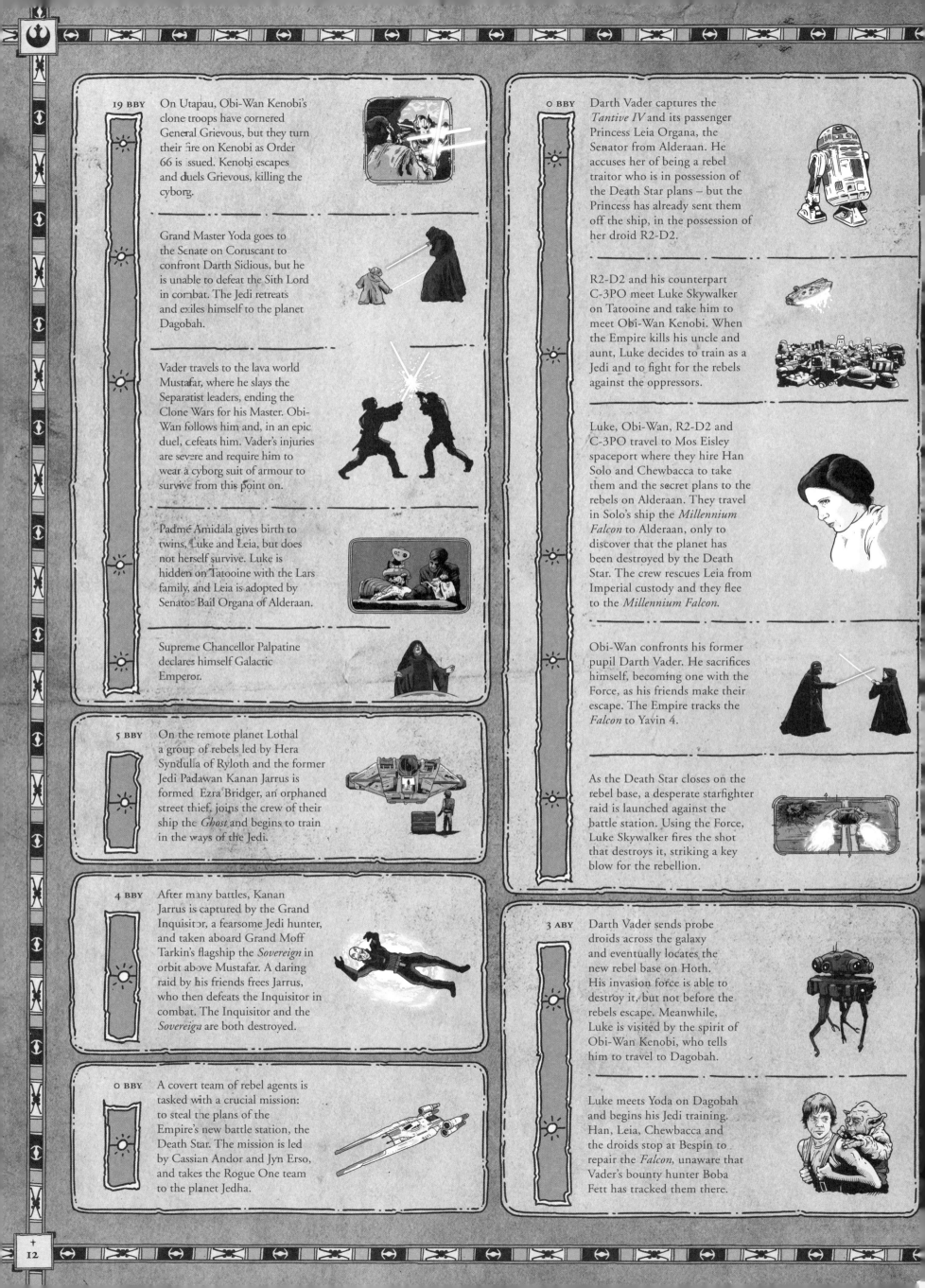

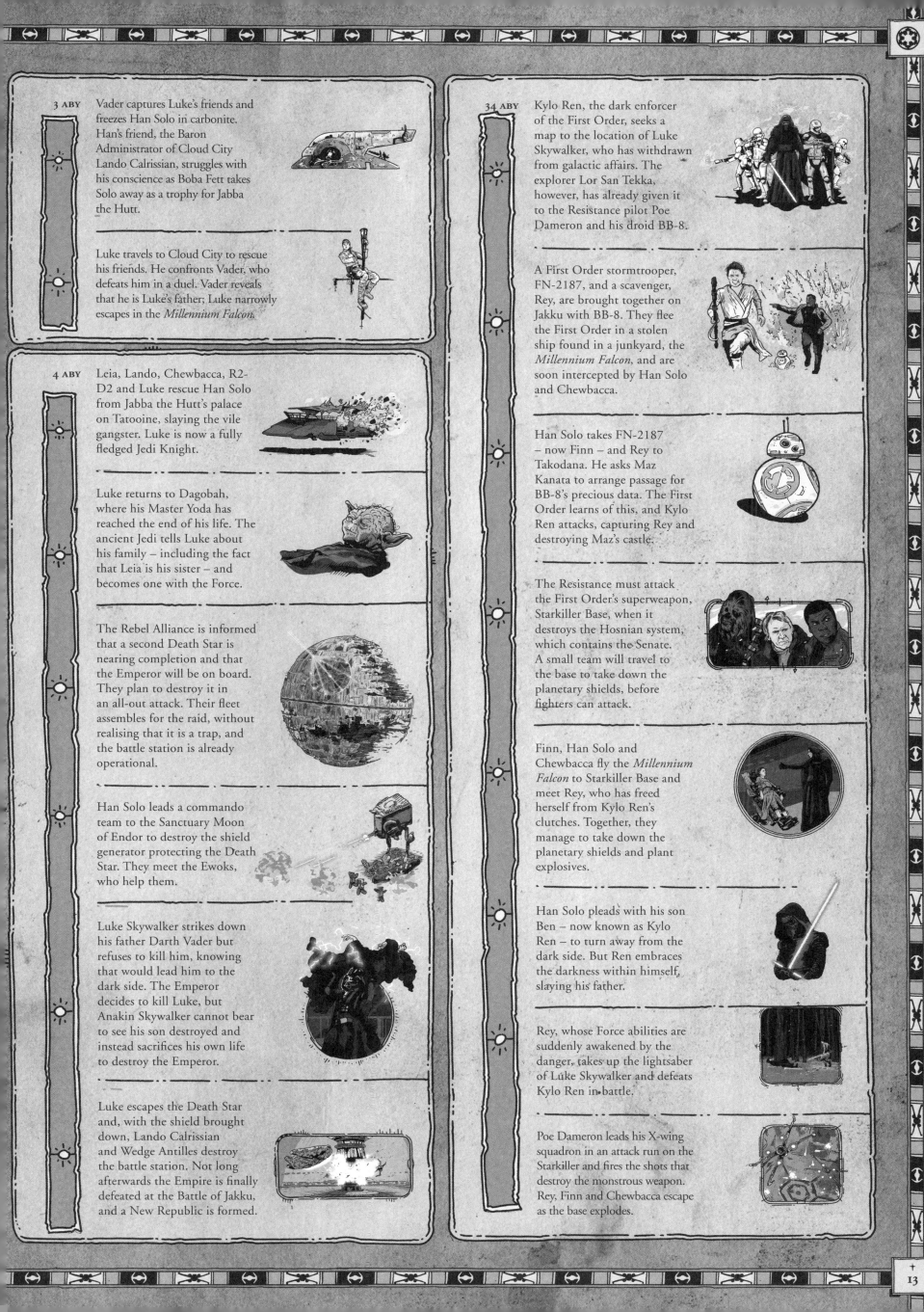

3 ABY

Vader captures Luke's friends and freezes Han Solo in carbonite. Han's friend, the Baron Administrator of Cloud City Lando Calrissian, struggles with his conscience as Boba Fett takes Solo away as a trophy for Jabba the Hutt.

Luke travels to Cloud City to rescue his friends. He confronts Vader, who defeats him in a duel. Vader reveals that he is Luke's father; Luke narrowly escapes in the *Millennium Falcon*.

4 ABY

Leia, Lando, Chewbacca, R2-D2 and Luke rescue Han Solo from Jabba the Hutt's palace on Tatooine, slaying the vile gangster. Luke is now a fully fledged Jedi Knight.

Luke returns to Dagobah, where his Master Yoda has reached the end of his life. The ancient Jedi tells Luke about his family – including the fact that Leia is his sister – and becomes one with the Force.

The Rebel Alliance is informed that a second Death Star is nearing completion and that the Emperor will be on board. They plan to destroy it in an all-out attack. Their fleet assembles for the raid, without realising that it is a trap, and the battle station is already operational.

Han Solo leads a commando team to the Sanctuary Moon of Endor to destroy the shield generator protecting the Death Star. They meet the Ewoks, who help them.

Luke Skywalker strikes down his father Darth Vader but refuses to kill him, knowing that would lead him to the dark side. The Emperor decides to kill Luke, but Anakin Skywalker cannot bear to see his son destroyed and instead sacrifices his own life to destroy the Emperor.

Luke escapes the Death Star and, with the shield brought down, Lando Calrissian and Wedge Antilles destroy the battle station. Not long afterwards the Empire is finally defeated at the Battle of Jakku, and a New Republic is formed.

34 ABY

Kylo Ren, the dark enforcer of the First Order, seeks a map to the location of Luke Skywalker, who has withdrawn from galactic affairs. The explorer Lor San Tekka, however, has already given it to the Resistance pilot Poe Dameron and his droid BB-8.

A First Order stormtrooper, FN-2187, and a scavenger, Rey, are brought together on Jakku with BB-8. They flee the First Order in a stolen ship found in a junkyard, the *Millennium Falcon*, and are soon intercepted by Han Solo and Chewbacca.

Han Solo takes FN-2187 – now Finn – and Rey to Takodana. He asks Maz Kanata to arrange passage for BB-8's precious data. The First Order learns of this, and Kylo Ren attacks, capturing Rey and destroying Maz's castle.

The Resistance must attack the First Order's superweapon, Starkiller Base, when it destroys the Hosnian system, which contains the Senate. A small team will travel to the base to take down the planetary shields, before fighters can attack.

Finn, Han Solo and Chewbacca fly the *Millennium Falcon* to Starkiller Base and meet Rey, who has freed herself from Kylo Ren's clutches. Together, they manage to take down the planetary shields and plant explosives.

Han Solo pleads with his son Ben – now known as Kylo Ren – to turn away from the dark side. But Ren embraces the darkness within himself, slaying his father.

Rey, whose Force abilities are suddenly awakened by the danger, takes up the lightsaber of Luke Skywalker and defeats Kylo Ren in battle.

Poe Dameron leads his X-wing squadron in an attack run on the Starkiller and fires the shots that destroy the monstrous weapon. Rey, Finn and Chewbacca escape as the base explodes.

HISTORICAL FIGURES

This turbulent period in the history of the galaxy produced many valiant heroes and terrifying villains. From the Clone Wars to the Galactic Civil War and beyond, here are some of the famous – and infamous – faces you will find in this book.

ADMIRAL ACKBAR

A legendary soldier and brilliant tactician, Ackbar rose to the rank of Admiral for the Alliance to Restore the Republic, commanding the rebel fleet. His exploits during the Clone Wars with the Mon Calamari Guard helped Prince Lee-Char to win the planet's throne and defeat a Separatist plot.

PADMÉ AMIDALA

The elected Queen and Senator from Naboo, Amidala fought desperately against the invading Trade Federation and brought the Jedi into the war. Her secret marriage to Anakin Skywalker ended tragically, as he fell to the dark side. A heartbroken Padmé died shortly after giving birth to Luke and Leia.

WEDGE ANTILLES

The rebel pilot Wedge Antilles had the distinction of helping to destroy not one but two Death Stars. He was one of the few survivors of the strike force at the Battle of Yavin and personally blew up the reactor of the second Death Star at Endor. He later flew crucial secret missions for the New Republic.

CAD BANE

The ruthless and deadly Duros bounty hunter was famed for his exploits during the Clone Wars – a daring holocron theft from the Jedi Temple, a prison break on Coruscant, and even the kidnap of the Republic's Supreme Chancellor, Palpatine. There was no job he would not take on – for the right price.

BB-8

The faithful companion to Resistance pilot Poe Dameron, BB-8, a spherical astromech droid, was entrusted with the map to Luke Skywalker by his master. After meeting Rey and Finn, he managed to succeed in his mission. BB-8 was a clever and resourceful droid, well aware of his ability to charm.

JAR JAR BINKS

Jar Jar Binks met Qui-Gon Jinn and Obi-Wan Kenobi during the invasion of Naboo and became friends with the Jedi and Queen Amidala, whom he helped to rescue. Later he became a representative for his planet in the Galactic Senate, unwittingly helping Chancellor Palpatine to seize absolute power.

EZRA BRIDGER

With his parents arrested by the Empire for rebellious activities, Ezra grew up on the streets of Lothal's Capital City, stealing to survive. A chance encounter with the former Jedi Kanan Jarrus and his Spectre cell led him to become Jarrus' apprentice and to become part of the early Rebel Alliance.

C-3PO

A protocol droid built from spare parts by Anakin Skywalker, in his childhood on Tatooine. C-3PO was fluent in over seven million forms of communication. Despite his anxious nature, C-3PO played a pivotal role in the Galactic Civil War, alongside his constant companion and counterpart R2-D2.

LANDO CALRISSIAN

The roguish gambler Lando Calrissian lost his ship the *Millennium Falcon* to his friend Han Solo in a game of sabacc. Later, as Baron Administrator of Cloud City, he betrayed Solo to the Empire but soon had a change of heart. General Calrissian helped the rebels destroy the second Death Star at the Battle of Endor.

CHEWBACCA

The legendary Wookiee Chewbacca fought for the Republic in the Clone Wars, and later gained fame as one of the heroes of the Battle of Yavin. He and his friend Han Solo became key figures in the rebellion. An ace pilot and engineer, he was also a mighty warrior and crack shot with his bowcaster.

POE DAMERON

Poe Dameron was an ace pilot for the Republic who was recruited by General Organa for her Resistance organisation. He helped to secure the map to the location of Luke Skywalker, despite the First Order capturing and interrogating him, and fired the shots that destroyed the Starkiller superweapon.

COUNT DOOKU

Dooku trained as the Padawan of Jedi Master Yoda and became a Master himself. He came to believe the Republic was corrupt and left to raise a Separatist army against it. As the Sith Lord Darth Tyranus, he was the apprentice of Darth Sidious, until his Master betrayed him. He was killed by Anakin Skywalker.

BOBA FETT

Boba was a clone of his 'father' Jango Fett, and as a boy witnessed his death at the hands of Jedi Master Mace Windu. He grew up to become one of the galaxy's most dangerous bounty hunters. Near the end of the Galactic Civil War, he fell into a sarlacc pit on Tatooine while working for Jabba the Hutt.

JANGO FETT

The galaxy's most feared bounty hunter, Jango Fett was chosen as the genetic template for the Republic's clone troopers as part of a plot by the Sith Lords Chancellor Palpatine and Count Dooku. He fought Obi-Wan Kenobi on Kamino and was killed during the Battle of Geonosis by Jedi Master Mace Windu.

FINN

Raised from infancy to be a stormtrooper by the First Order, FN-2187 was a model soldier until his first combat mission. He refused to fire on innocent people and fled the First Order with the Resistance pilot Poe Dameron, who gave him the name Finn. He then helped his new friends destroy Starkiller Base.

GRAND INQUISITOR

Inquisitors were dark-side-using Jedi hunters, employed by Emperor Palpatine to seek out survivors of Order 66. The Grand Inquisitor was sent to the planet Lothal to find Kanan Jarrus, but after a series of battles Jarrus defeated him in a duel aboard the Star Destroyer *Sovereign*, and he was destroyed.

GENERAL GRIEVOUS

The Kaleesh warrior Grievous was a fearsome cyborg, with almost all of his original body replaced with mechanical 'upgrades'. Trained in lightsaber combat by Count Dooku, he became a key Separatist general, commanding vast droid armies. He was killed by Obi-Wan Kenobi near the end of the Clone Wars.

JABBA THE HUTT

The vile gangster ruled a criminal empire from his palace on Tatooine. After a bounty hunter brought him Han Solo, the Hutt's former employee, Jabba hung him frozen in carbonite on the wall of his throne room. It was during the smuggler's rescue by Luke Skywalker that the Hutt was slain by Princess Leia.

KANAN JARRUS

Caleb Dume was only a Padawan learner when Order 66 happened, and his Master Depa Billaba was killed helping him escape. Taking the name Kanan Jarrus he fled his old life, until events forced him to take up his lightsaber once more. His rebel cell became a serious threat to the Empire.

QUI-GON JINN

A powerful and unusual Jedi Master, Qui-Gon Jinn was trained by Count Dooku and in turn was the Master of Obi-Wan Kenobi. He learned the secret of maintaining his consciousness after death, a power he passed on to Yoda and Kenobi. Jinn was slain by the Sith Darth Maul during the invasion of Naboo.

OBI-WAN KENOBI

Famed as a wise negotiator and cunning warrior, Obi-Wan Kenobi fought with intelligence and courage in the Clone Wars. With the rise of the Empire, he took it upon himself to watch over Luke Skywalker and trained him as a Jedi. He sacrificed himself against Darth Vader to save Luke, but his spirit lived on.

LOBOT

Lobot had cybernetic implants put into his brain by the Empire, enabling him to run complex calculations for them. Later, while helping Lando to steal Emperor Palpatine's yacht, he was seriously injured, and his cyborg brain took over. He helped the crew of the *Millennium Falcon* escape Cloud City.

DARTH MAUL

Maul, a Zabrak from Dathomir, was born to Talzin of the Nightsisters but kidnapped by Darth Sidious as a child. Through years of cruel training he became a devastating Sith warrior and slew the Jedi Master Qui-Gon Jinn. He was then maimed by Obi-Wan Kenobi, only to rise again as a cyborg crime lord.

MON MOTHMA

Mon Mothma was Senator for the planet Chandrila during the Clone Wars, but as Supreme Chancellor Palpatine tightened his grip on power she began to form a network of resistance. She became a key leader in the Alliance to Restore the Republic and later served as the first Chancellor of the New Republic.

HONDO OHNAKA

Hondo was a cunning Weequay pirate and leader of the Ohnaka Gang, operating from the Outer Rim planet Florrum. They engaged in kidnapping for ransom, robbery, black-market arms trading and extortion. A born survivor, he lived through clashes with the Jedi, the Separatists, and even Darth Maul.

SAVAGE OPRESS

Savage was a Nightbrother warrior who was infused with dark magicks by his mother Talzin and transformed into a monstrous warrior. He learned the dark side as an apprentice under Count Dooku and later his brother Maul. The brothers duelled Darth Sidious, who defeated them and slew Opress.

ZEB ORRELIOS

The Empire brutally massacred the Lasat people, from the Outer Rim world Lasan. One of the few survivors was Garazeb Orrelios, a member of the Lasan Honour Guard. A formidable warrior, the gruff but good-hearted Orrelios became a member of a rebel cell which came together on Lothal.

LEIA ORGANA

Leia was raised by her adoptive parents on Alderaan as a princess and grew up to become both a Senator and a rebel leader. Her real father, Darth Vader, never knew the truth. After winning the Galactic Civil War, Leia married Han Solo and led the Resistance against the sinister First Order.

PALPATINE

Born on Naboo, Sheev Palpatine became a Senator, and, through clever political scheming, Supreme Chancellor. Secretly, he was Sidious, Dark Lord of the Sith, controlling both sides in the Clone Wars and seizing absolute power as Emperor. He was destroyed by his former pupil Anakin Skywalker.

CAPTAIN PHASMA

Alongside General Hux and Kylo Ren, Captain Phasma was one of the key commanders of the First Order. She was in charge of training stormtroopers and led them into battle herself. Her distinctive armour was coated with chromium salvaged from a starship once owned by Emperor Palpatine himself.

R2-D2

Heroic astromech droid R2-D2 witnessed some of the galaxy's most crucial events, from the invasion of Naboo and the Clone Wars to the rise and fall of the Galactic Empire. He accompanied both Anakin and Luke Skywalker on adventures and was key to efforts to destroy the Death Star.

KYLO REN

At his birth, the son of Han Solo and Leia Organa was named 'Ben'. His Jedi training with Luke Skywalker ended in tragedy when, seduced by the dark side, he betrayed the other students and was responsible for their destruction. As Kylo Ren, the First Order's enforcer, he killed his father on Starkiller Base.

REY

Rey grew up on the planet Jakku, where she had been left at an early age. She scavenged the ship graveyard for parts to trade to her guardian, the junkboss Unkar Plutt, and waited for her family. A chance encounter with a Resistance droid led her to leave the planet and discover her destiny as a Jedi.

ANAKIN SKYWALKER

Anakin Skywalker was discovered as a child slave on the planet Tatooine by the Jedi Master Qui-Gon Jinn. His incredible potential led to him being trained as a Jedi, and he became one of the Republic's greatest heroes. However, he came under the sway of the Sith Lord Darth Sidious and fell to the dark side.

LUKE SKYWALKER

The farm boy from Tatooine who longed for the stars became one of the galaxy's most important figures. The last Jedi Knight, trained by Obi-Wan Kenobi and Yoda, joined the Rebel Alliance, turned his father Anakin Skywalker back to the light, and overthrew the Emperor. Later, he withdrew from galactic affairs.

HAN SOLO

A smuggler, rogue, famed pilot and crack shot, Han Solo became caught up in the Galactic Civil War when he was hired to take Obi-Wan Kenobi and Luke Skywalker to Alderaan. He joined the rebels, helped to win the war, married Princess Leia, but was then tragically struck down by his son, Ben.

HERA SYNDULLA

The daughter of famed Twi'lek freedom fighter Cham Syndulla, Hera grew up on her home planet Ryloth as the Clone Wars and Imperial occupation ravaged it. Hera decided to leave Ryloth in her ship the *Ghost* to fight the Empire and became a founding member of a rebel cell based on Lothal.

MOTHER TALZIN

The leader of Dathomir's Nightsisters, Mother Talzin was a powerful sorceress who wielded the dark side of the Force. She plotted both with and against the Sith Lords Sidious and Tyranus, who eventually sent Grievous to destroy her clan. She was killed saving her son Maul from Palpatine and Dooku.

AHSOKA TANO

Grand Master Yoda assigned this young but talented Togruta Jedi to Anakin Skywalker as his Padawan learner. She served heroically in the Clone Wars, before a sinister plot led her to leave the Order. Later, as the agent 'Fulcrum', she helped establish a network of rebels against Imperial tyranny.

WILHUFF TARKIN

Ruthlessly ambitious and highly intelligent, Wilhuff Tarkin rose through the ranks of the Imperial military to become one of the most powerful men in the galaxy. As Grand Moff, he commanded the first Death Star, destroying the planet Alderaan. He was killed when the battle station exploded.

LOR SAN TEKKA

Lor San Tekka was an explorer who was fascinated by the legends of the Jedi and became a member of the Church of the Force which kept Jedi ideals alive in the age of the Empire. He possessed a map that could help to locate Luke Skywalker and gave it to the Resistance before Kylo Ren struck him down.

SHAAK TI

The Togruta Jedi Master Shaak Ti was a member of the High Council during the Clone Wars and was responsible for the training of the Republic's clone army on the planet Kamino. Though a skilled and cunning warrior, she was killed by Darth Vader during the Jedi Purge as she meditated in the Temple.

LUMINARA UNDULI

A member of the Jedi High Council, Luminara Unduli was one of the most highly respected Jedi Masters of her time. Following the victory of Emperor Palpatine over the Jedi, Unduli was executed on Stygeon Prime, and her remains used as a trap to draw in survivors of Order 66.

DARTH VADER

When Anakin Skywalker turned to the dark side, his new Master dubbed him Darth Vader. Terribly injured on Mustafar, he was sealed into cyborg life-support armour and served the Emperor as his feared right hand. At the last, he turned on his Master, destroying him to save the life of his son, Luke Skywalker.

ASAJJ VENTRESS

Born on Dathomir into the Force-using clan of Nightsisters, Ventress was apprenticed to the Sith Lord Count Dooku and became his assassin. Dooku and Ventress eventually tried to kill each other, and she struck out on her own as a bounty hunter. She died heroically, protecting the Jedi Quinlan Vos.

MACE WINDU

Jedi Master Mace Windu was known as one of the Order's greatest champions – his skill with a lightsaber and the Force was almost unmatched. He fought many key battles of the Clone Wars as a general, including the raid on Geonosis. He was killed by Darth Sidious while trying to arrest the Sith Lord.

SABINE WREN

Sabine Wren was born into the Mandalorian warrior tradition. As a child she joined the Imperial Academy as a cadet. However, the Empire's oppression led her to flee her home planet and join a cell of rebels on the planet Lothal. She was a weapons and explosives expert and keen artist.

YODA

The Grand Master of the Jedi Council was the wisest and most powerful of them all. He failed, however, to uncover the Sith Lord Sidious and arrogantly chose to face him in single combat. After Palpatine fought him to a standstill, Yoda retreated into exile, where he eventually trained Luke Skywalker.

ABAFAR
TO
YAVIN 4

ABAFAR: A barren world rich in rhydonium. During the Clone Wars the Separatists loaded a stolen freighter with this explosive and tried to use it to blow up a top Republic military conference. They were thwarted by D-Squad, a covert team of droids under Colonel Meebur Gascon.

DANTOOINE: Once used by the Rebel Alliance as a base, it was the location given by Princess Leia to Grand Moff Tarkin when he demanded she reveal their headquarters. Because Dantooine was too remote to serve as a demonstration of the Death Star's power, Tarkin targeted Alderaan instead.

DATHOMIR: A mysterious world of jungles, swamps and mountains, haunted by witches and rancors. Dathomir's Nightsisters were one of the known groups of Force-users who were not Jedi or Sith until conflict with Darth Tyranus and Darth Sidious led to one of their clans being massacred.

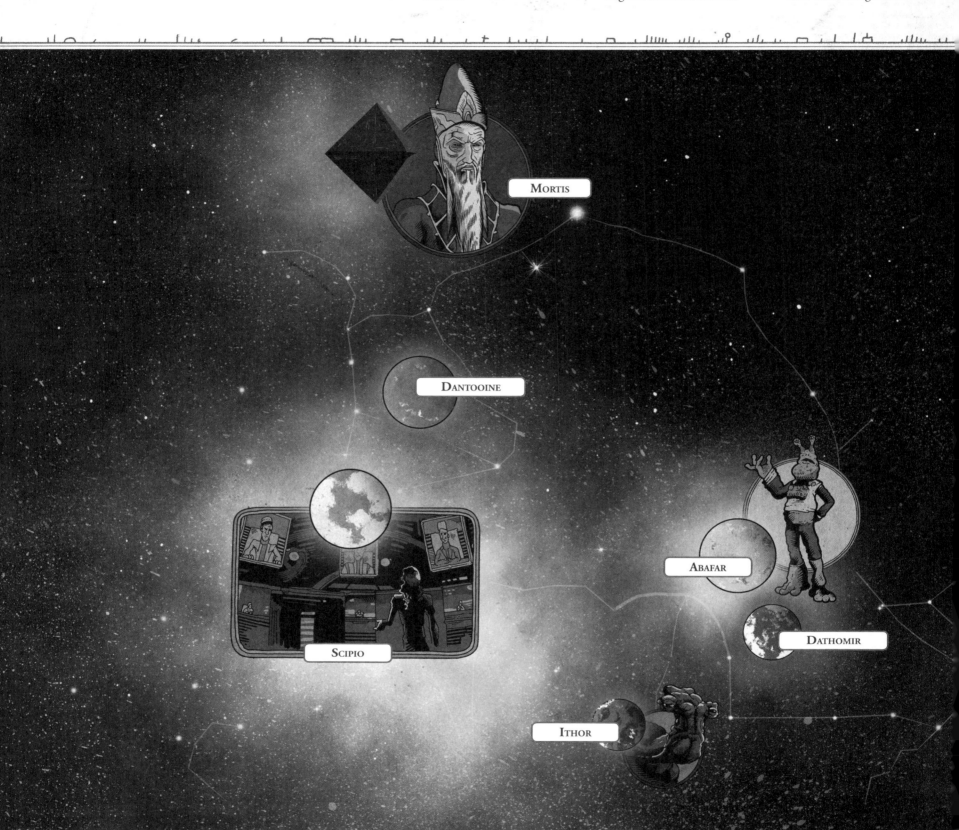

MON CALA: The vast oceans of Mon Cala are home to the Mon Calamari and Quarren species. A bitter struggle between the two led to them taking opposite sides during the Clone Wars. The Republic defeated the Separatists; Lee-Char of the Mon Calamari proved himself in battle, becoming King.

The planet suffered under the Empire, and the Mon Calamari became key allies of the rebels. Admiral Ackbar was commander of the rebel fleet at the Battle of Endor.

Mon Calamari ships were some of the largest and most powerful in the rebel fleet.

MORABAND: The desolate homeworld of the Sith holds many evil secrets. In the Valley of the Dark Lords the tombs of powerful Sith are haunted by the presence of the dark side; Yoda travelled here as part of his quest to discover the secret of immortality and encountered a vision of Darth Bane.

MORTIS: Discovered by the Jedi Anakin Skywalker, Mortis is a mysterious realm resembling a bizarre planet whose landscape changes constantly. It was home to three powerful 'Force wielders', the Daughter, the Son and the Father, who represented the light, the dark and balance respectively.

QUERMIA: Home to the Quermian species – tall, pale humanoids with long necks and two pairs of arms.

Quermian Jedi Master Yarael Poof was a respected member of the Jedi Council, known for his skill with diplomacy, illusions and mind tricks.

FELUCIA: Felucia's position in the middle of an important hyperspace lane made it a key target during the Clone Wars. Many battles were fought for control of it. The planet itself is a farm world with great jungles of fungus. It is noted for its production of the valuable healing herb nysillin.

ITHOR: The peaceful Ithorian people, sometimes known as 'hammerheads', tend to the sacred jungles of their homeworlds. They are known for their remarkable farming technology; the Galactic Empire forced them to reveal their secrets in return for sparing the planet a devastating invasion.

JELUCAN: A world of ice and towering mountain peaks. Jelucan was settled in two waves of colonists: the second-wavers became rich miners, while the first-wavers clung to their more rigid mountain traditions. It was notable as the homeworld of star-crossed lovers Thane Kyrell and Ciena Ree.

LOLA SAYU: From orbit, Lola Sayu is a purple jewel of a planet. It is volcanic, with a cracked surface through which lakes of lava bubble up. It was once the site of a Jedi prison called the Citadel. When the Separatists took over the planet, they used it to hold Jedi prisoners of their own.

MARIDUN: A grass-covered planet, home to the peace-loving Lurmen. It was used to test a new Separatist weapon: the Defoliator, which destroyed life but not technology – like the Separatists' battle droids. The scheme was foiled by the Jedi Anakin Skywalker, Ahsoka Tano and Aayla Secura.

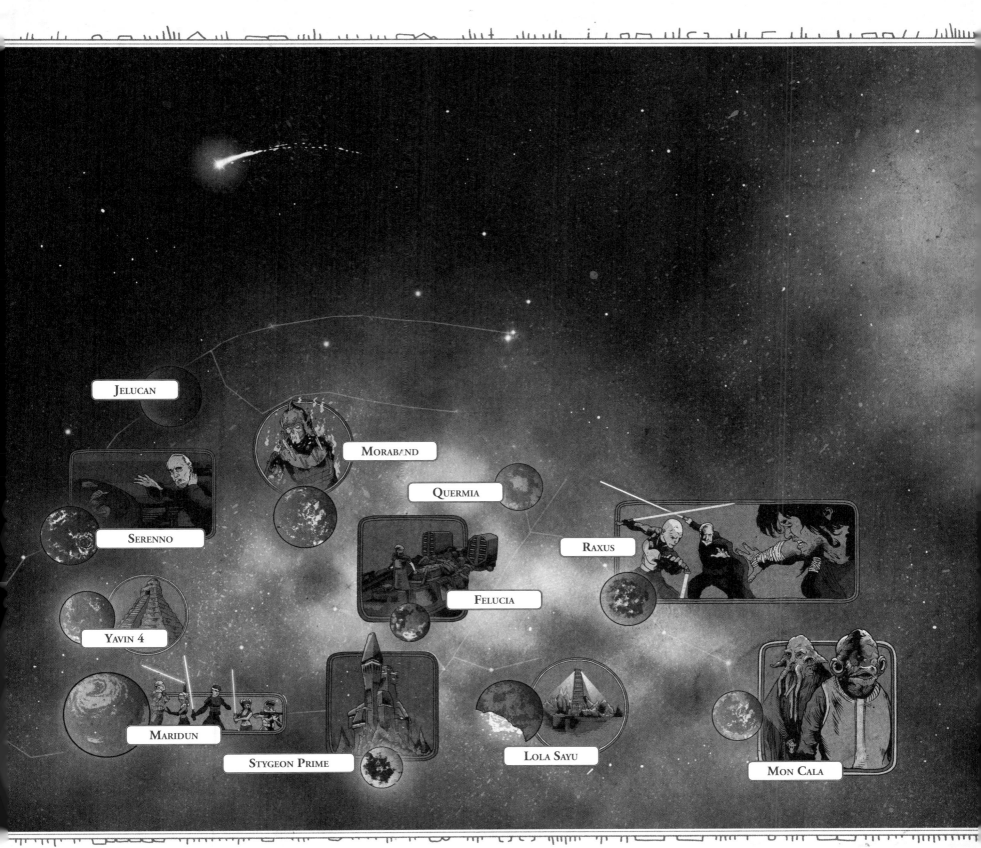

RAXUS: The capital of the Confederacy of Independent Systems during the Clone Wars, Raxus is a beautiful world of forests, plains and oceans.

From here, Count Dooku sparked the Separatist Crisis that led to the Clone Wars and the fall of the Republic.

SCIPIO: The InterGalactic Banking Clan was one of the most important organisations in the Outer Rim, based on the icy planet Scipio. During the Clone Wars this key Separatist planet was captured by the Republic, giving Chancellor Palpatine control of the galaxy's largest banking system.

SERENNO: A forested world that was home to Count Dooku, one of the central figures of the Clone Wars. An aristocrat who gave up his title to join the Jedi Order, he later became disillusioned and left to form the Separatists. He was also, secretly, Darth Tyranus, apprentice to Darth Sidious.

STYGEON PRIME: The snow-capped mountains of Stygeon Prime hid the high-security prison known as the Spire. Darth Sidious imprisoned his former apprentice Maul here, and kept the remains of Jedi Master Luminara Unduli here to lure in any Jedi who survived the Order's destruction.

YAVIN 4: The small jungle moon which served as a base for the Rebel Alliance for their assault on the first Death Star.

The location of the rebel base here was the crucial secret held back by the rebel leader and Senator Leia Organa during her interrogation by Darth Vader.

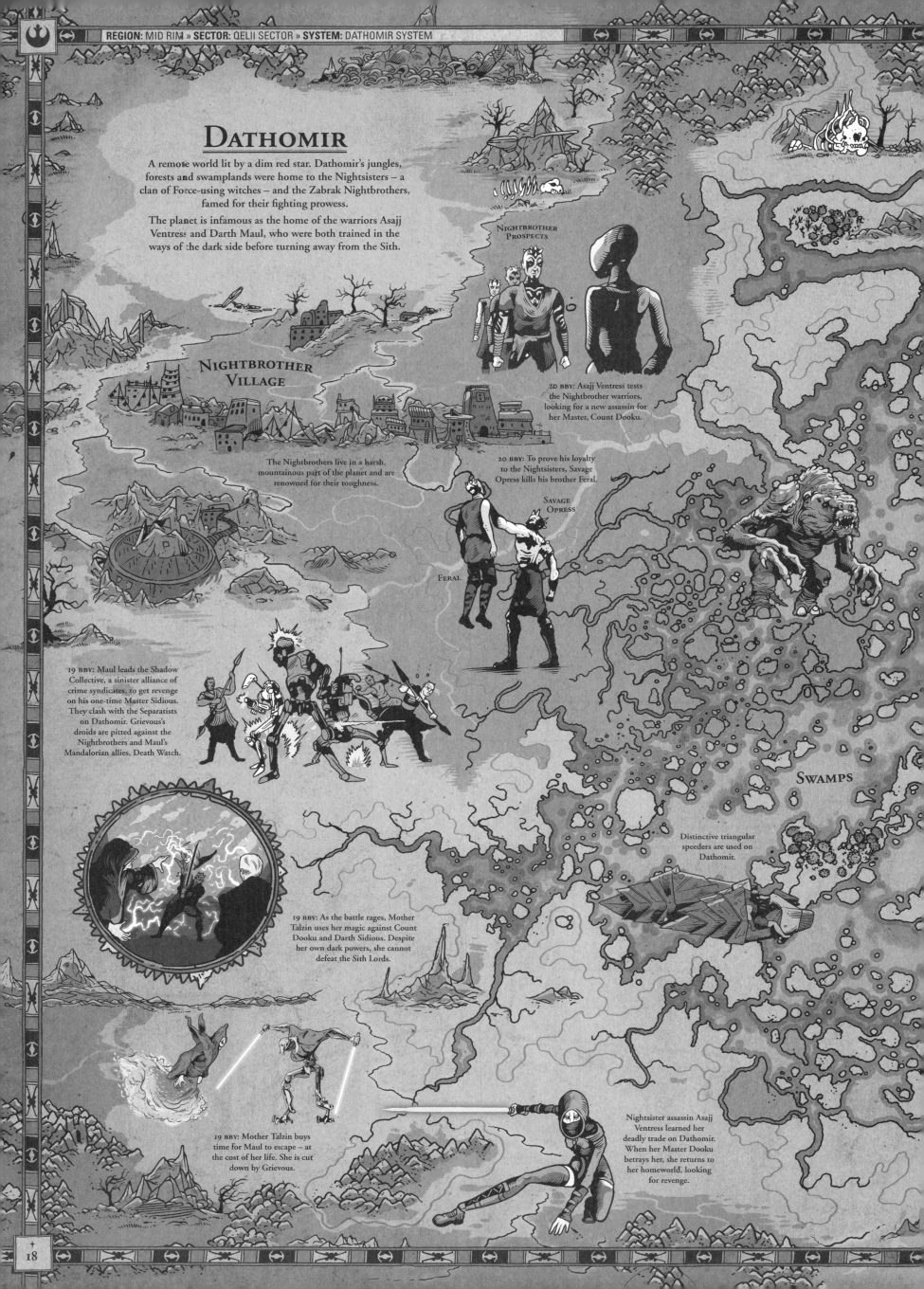

DATHOMIR

A remote world lit by a dim red star. Dathomir's jungles, forests and swamplands were home to the Nightsisters – a clan of Force-using witches – and the Zabrak Nightbrothers, famed for their fighting prowess.

The planet is infamous as the home of the warriors Asajj Ventress and Darth Maul, who were both trained in the ways of the dark side before turning away from the Sith.

NIGHTBROTHER
PROSPECTS

20 BBY: Asajj Ventress tests the Nightbrother warriors, looking for a new assassin for her Master, Count Dooku.

NIGHTBROTHER VILLAGE

The Nightbrothers live in a harsh, mountainous part of the planet and are renowned for their toughness.

20 BBY: To prove his loyalty to the Nightsisters, Savage Opress kills his brother Feral.

SAVAGE OPRESS

FERAL

19 BBY: Maul leads the Shadow Collective, a sinister alliance of crime syndicates, to get revenge on his one-time Master Sidious. They clash with the Separatists on Dathomir. Grievous's droids are pitted against the Nightbrothers and Maul's Mandalorian allies, Death Watch.

SWAMPS

Distinctive triangular speeders are used on Dathomir.

19 BBY: As the battle rages, Mother Talzin uses her magic against Count Dooku and Darth Sidious. Despite her own dark powers, she cannot defeat the Sith Lords.

19 BBY: Mother Talzin buys time for Maul to escape – at the cost of her life. She is cut down by Grievous.

Nightsister assassin Asajj Ventress learned her deadly trade on Dathomir. When her Master Dooku betrays her, she returns to her homeworld, looking for revenge.

Darth Sidious travels to Dathomir to share dark side wisdom with Mother Talzin, leader of the Nightsisters. He takes her son Maul and raises him as his apprentice.

MAUL

20 BBY: Tired of Asajj Ventress's failures against the Jedi, Count Dooku seeks a new assassin. He asks Mother Talzin for help, little knowing that she is plotting with Ventress to kill him.

FOREST

NIGHTSISTER VILLAGE

The witches of Dathomir have many uncanny and terrifying powers.

OLD DAKA

20 BBY: When the Nightsisters attempt to kill Count Dooku, he sends Grievous and his droids to destroy them.

20 BBY: The sorceress Old Daka raises an army of undead Nightsisters to attack Grievous' forces.

20 BBY: Despite the army of undead, General Grievous slays Old Daka and his troops take the Nightsister village. Only Talzin and Ventress escape.

20 BBY: Maul's brother Savage Opress is infused with dark magic and becomes a mighty and terrifying warrior. He will become Dooku's new assassin – but Talzin plots to use him against the Count.

20 BBY: Obi-Wan and Anakin arrive to investigate the 'monster', Savage Opress, who is killing Jedi.

Huge, terrifying, semi-intelligent rancors are native to Dathomir.

20 BBY: Years after his supposed death, Darth Maul returns to Dathomir. Talzin replaces his bizarre cyborg spider-legs with more humanoid ones.

0 ABY: Jyn Erso is tasked with a crucial mission by the Rebel Alliance: to steal the plans of the Empire's secret weapon, the Death Star.

Elegant whisper birds roost in Yavin's treetops.

WHISPER BIRD

YAVIN 4

The forested fourth moon of the red gas giant Yavin is known for its mysterious monuments and great stepped temples, which sheltered the forces of the Alliance to Restore the Republic during the early days of the Galactic Civil War. The moon – and the hopes of the rebellion – would have been annihilated if not for the destruction of the Death Star.

PIRANHA BEETLE

Carnivorous piranha beetles can be deadly in large swarms.

Stintarils are a species of rodent that hunts in packs. They are known to prey on whisper birds.

STINTARIL

Bulbous anglers dangle their limbs in the swamps, waiting for food to absorb.

ANGLER

LIZARD CRAB

Armoured eels lurk in the swamps, fishing for lizard crabs.

Lizard crabs are native to Yavin 4's swamps and are preyed on by many creatures.

ARMOURED EEL

Vast leviathan grubs burrow for years beneath the moon's dense forests, feeding on tree roots.

Leviathan Grub

5 ABY: Rebel pilots Kes Dameron and Shara Bey settle here in the aftermath of the Galactic Civil War. They plant a Force-sensitive tree, one of the last such trees in the galaxy.

Brightly coloured woolamanders live in the forest canopy.

Woolamander

Runyip

Plant-eating runyips forage on the forest floor. They are often harassed by piranha beetles.

0 ABY: The heroes of the Battle of Yavin are honoured in a ceremony at the headquarters of the Rebel Alliance.

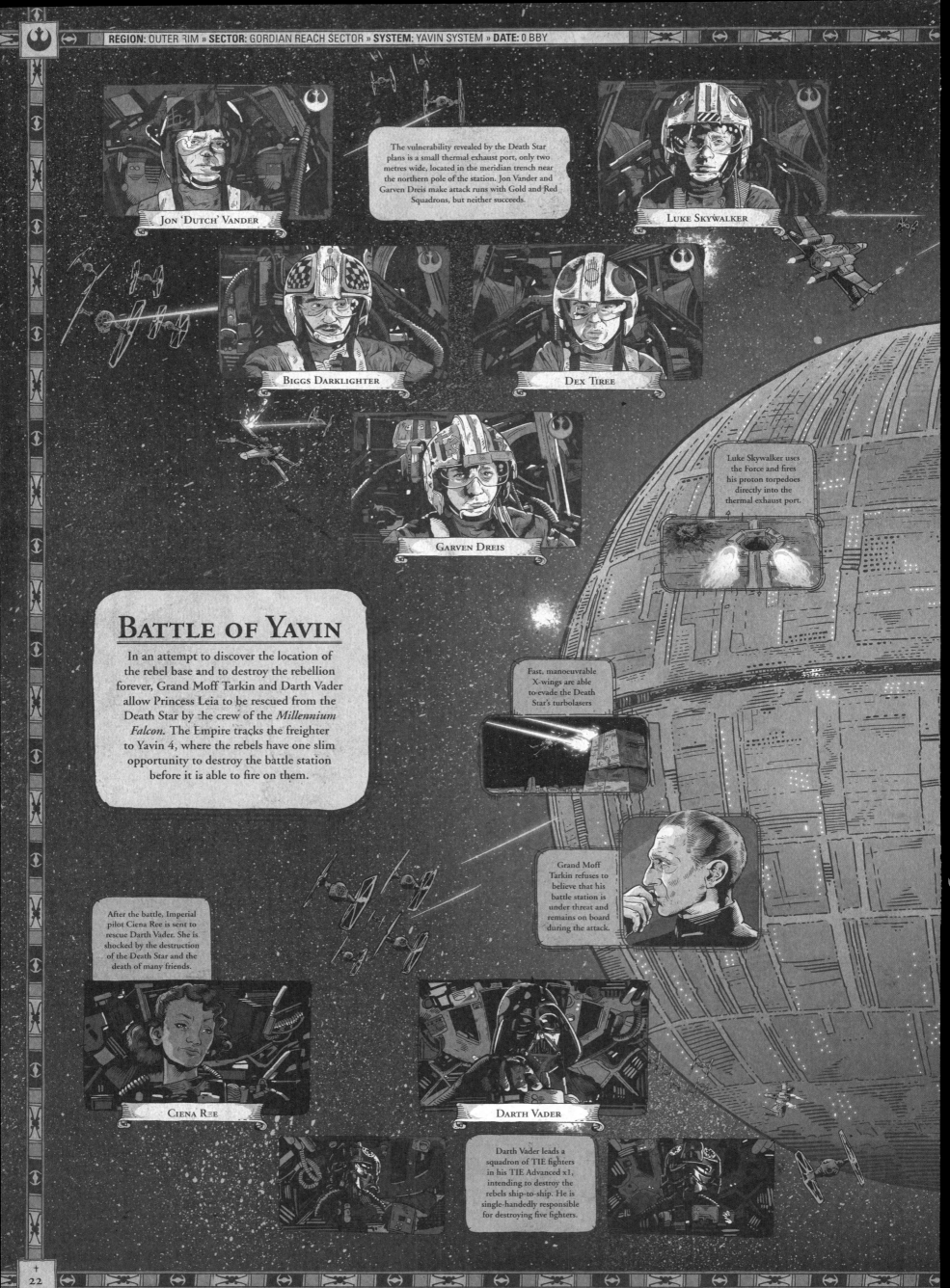

JON 'DUTCH' VANDER

The vulnerability revealed by the Death Star plans is a small thermal exhaust port, only two metres wide, located in the meridian trench near the northern pole of the station. Jon Vander and Garven Dreis make attack runs with Gold and Red Squadrons, but neither succeeds.

LUKE SKYWALKER

BIGGS DARKLIGHTER

DEX TIREE

GARVEN DREIS

Luke Skywalker uses the Force and fires his proton torpedoes directly into the thermal exhaust port.

BATTLE OF YAVIN

In an attempt to discover the location of the rebel base and to destroy the rebellion forever, Grand Moff Tarkin and Darth Vader allow Princess Leia to be rescued from the Death Star by the crew of the *Millennium Falcon*. The Empire tracks the freighter to Yavin 4, where the rebels have one slim opportunity to destroy the battle station before it is able to fire on them.

Fast, manoeuvrable X-wings are able to evade the Death Star's turbolasers

Grand Moff Tarkin refuses to believe that his battle station is under threat and remains on board during the attack.

After the battle, Imperial pilot Ciena Ree is sent to rescue Darth Vader. She is shocked by the destruction of the Death Star and the death of many friends.

CIENA REE

DARTH VADER

Darth Vader leads a squadron of TIE fighters in his TIE Advanced x1, intending to destroy the rebels ship-to-ship. He is single-handedly responsible for destroying five fighters.

WEDGE ANTILLES

THERON NETT

With Darth Vader wreaking havoc on the rebel starfighters, it falls to Luke Skywalker to make the final trench run. As he nears his target, with his wingman Wedge Antilles forced to break off his attack, he is spoken to from beyond the grave by the spirit of his Master, Obi-Wan Kenobi.

EVAAN VERLAINE

JEK TONO PORKINS

DAVISH 'POPS' KRAIL

YAVIN

With Darth Vader about to destroy Luke Skywalker's X-wing, the *Millennium Falcon* swoops in to save the rebel pilot.

YAVIN 4

On Yavin 4, General Dodonna and Princess Leia wait anxiously for news of the assault as the Death Star prepares to fire on them.

NEW CORAL CITY

SCUBA clone troopers arrive to help the Mon Calamari in their battle against the Quarrens.

While most of the population lives in underwater cities, some cities are built entirely or partially above the waves.

MON CALA

Mon Cala is a strategically important ocean world inhabited by two aquatic species, the Mon Calamari and the Quarren. During the Imperial era the planet suffered under occupation and began to provide secret support to the Alliance to Restore the Republic in the form of ships as well as soldiers like Admiral Ackbar.

With the tide of battle turning in favour of the Separatists, the Republic calls in a squad of Gungans from Naboo.

CAPTAIN ACKBAR'S MON CALAMARI GUARD

ANAKIN SKYWALKER

AHSOKA TANO

The Jedi Council sends clone troops and Jedi, including Anakin Skywalker and Ahsoka Tano, to help against the Separatists.

Captain Ackbar and his Mon Calamari Guard rally to support Prince Lee-Char against the Quarren and their Separatist allies.

Anakin uses the Force to collapse the central Planetary Scanner so that Republic reinforcements can land.

King Yos Kolina asks the Republic and the Jedi for help against the Separatists. Soon after, he is assassinated by Riff Tamson, a Separatist Commander.

Prince Lee-Char faces his father's assassin Riff Tamson in single combat and slays the fearsome Karkarodon commander.

KING KOLINA

RIFF TAMSON

PRINCE LEE-CHAR

Master Kit Fisto defends Prince Lee-Char from Riff Tamson – he is captured, but the Prince escapes.

MON CALA EEL

KIT FISTO

The Separatists send in aqua droids to reinforce the Quarren troops, causing massive casualties.

With King Kolina dead, the Quarren refuse to let the young and inexperienced Prince Lee-Char become their new ruler. The long peace between them and the Mon Calamari breaks down into civil war.

QUARREN WARRIOR

As the civil war between the Mon Cala and the Quarren rages, the Separatists attack in Trident assault ships.

TRIDENT ASSAULT SHIP

Riff Tamson and the Quarren chieftain Nossor Ri receive their orders from Count Dooku.

Anakin, Kit Fisto, Padmé Amidala and Jar Jar Binks are captured but later escape

MORTIS

During the Clone Wars, Anakin Skywalker, Obi-Wan Kenobi and Ahsoka Tano are drawn through a bizarre portal into the world of Mortis – a world seemingly fashioned from the Force itself. They encounter the Father, a Force Wielder who keeps the balance between his children, the Daughter and the Son. The Father intends to test Anakin, to discover if he is truly the Chosen One ...

The Son and the Daughter are capable of transforming into huge, winged beasts.

THE DAUGHTER

Obi-Wan, Anakin and Ahsoka explore the lush, beautiful landscape of Mortis. It is strong with the Force and strangely unnatural, with its floating islands of rock.

Obi-Wan and Anakin have strange visions inside a mountain cave. Obi-Wan is visited by the spirit of his old Master, Qui-Gon Jinn.

Ahsoka is killed by the Son. The Daughter channels her life force through Anakin to revive her.

THE FATHER

The Son shows Anakin a glimpse of his future, including the terrible fate that awaits him as Darth Vader. Later, the Father erases Anakin's memory of this vision.

The Father keeps the balance between the Daughter and the Son. He destroys himself with the Dagger of Mortis to prevent the Son from triumphing.

The Son, transformed into a winged beast, kidnaps Ahsoka Tano.

THE SON

In an underground chamber lies the Altar of Mortis. It held the Dagger of Mortis – the only weapon capable of killing the Father, the Son or the Daughter.

Ahsoka is kidnapped by the Son and infected with the dark side of the Force. Filled with rage, she is turned against Obi-Wan and Anakin as they fight the Son for the Dagger.

Alderaan to Teth

ALDERAAN: Known for its stunning natural beauty, Alderaan was one of the oldest members of the Galactic Republic, a peaceful world whose people valued art and culture. Because of its leaders' secret support for the Rebel Alliance, it was destroyed by the Empire using the Death Star.

ANTAR 4: Scene of the infamous Antar Atrocity carried out by Grand Moff Tarkin as a warning to former Separatists.

BALNAB: A primitive world once visited by C-3PO and R2-D2. The planet's ruler was a hologram created by a group of stranded pit droids.

CORELLIA: An important Core World known for its ships and pilots. Han Solo and Wedge Antilles were born here, and the Corellian Engineering Corporation manufactured the YT-1300 light freighter the *Millennium Falcon*, known as one of the fastest ships in the galaxy.

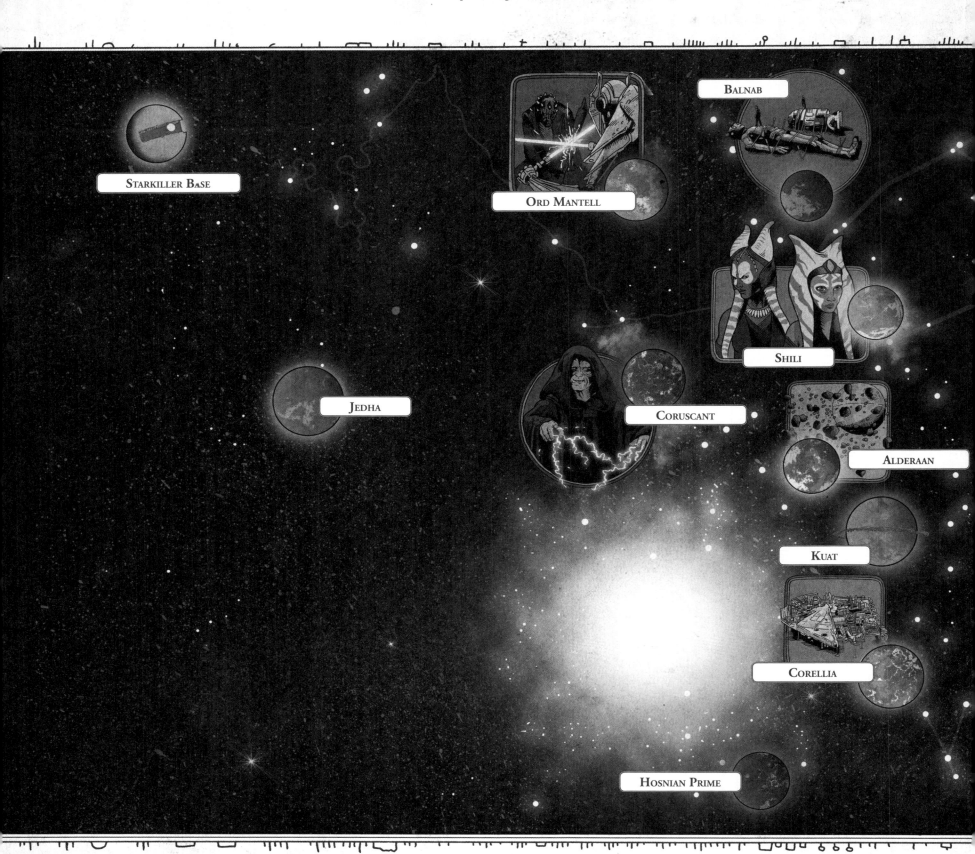

STARKILLER BASE

BALNAB

ORD MANTELL

SHILI

JEDHA

CORUSCANT

ALDERAAN

KUAT

CORELLIA

HOSNIAN PRIME

KUAT: The shipyards of Kuat are famous throughout the galaxy; it was here that the Republic's *Acclamator* assault ships and the Empire's Star Destroyers were built. A vast man-made ring of factories and spacedocks encircles the planet, allowing huge vehicles to be built in orbit.

LOTHAL: A quiet and peaceful agricultural world known for its jogan fruit, Lothal at first welcomed the Galactic Empire. However, the Empire soon began to oppress and exploit Lothal, strip-mining it for minerals. A famous cell of rebels formed here and won notable victories against the Empire.

MANDALORE: The Mandalorian people were once renowned as fierce and deadly warriors, The New Mandalorians, however, have tried to put the violence of the past behind them. They are opposed by terrorists like Death Watch, operating from their exile on Mandalore's moon Concordia.

ONDERON: Onderon's thick jungles are inhabited by deadly creatures. The humans on the planet live in cities protected by thick walls, such as the capital city Iziz. A key rebel leader, Saw Gerrera, waged a guerrilla campaign here against the occupying Separatist forces with the help of the Jedi.

ORD MANTELL: A mountainous world covered by thick, pinkish clouds and inhabited by Falleen and humans, Ord Mantell is well known as a base of the Black Sun gang. During the Clone Wars, Maul's Shadow Collective took over the Black Sun and fought a battle here against the Separatists.

CORUSCANT: Capital of the Republic and later the Galactic Empire. It is a planet covered by a vast city of skyscrapers, rising miles into the sky.

After the Galactic Civil War the Galactic Senate of the New Republic moved from system to system on a rotating basis.

GAREL: Briefly the hiding place of the rebel cell led by Hera Syndulla and Kanan Jarrus, during the Imperial years.

GORSE: A mining world, with one side permanently in darkness and the other in blazing sunlight. Kanan Jarrus met Hera Syndulla here.

HOSNIAN PRIME: With the Empire defeated, a New Republic rose from the ashes. Its capital was changed by election every few years, and while the Senate was based on Hosnian Prime the First Order used Starkiller Base to destroy the system, the Senate, and much of the Republic fleet.

JEDHA: An ancient world, dusty Jedha was once a place of holy pilgrimage. During Imperial occupation, extremist rebel Saw Gerrera had a hideout here.

KASHYYYK: The Wookiee homeworld, known for its majestic wroshyr trees. Cities spiral around their huge trunks.

KESSEL: One side of this world is lush and beautiful: elegant palaces and their exquisitely tended grounds sit among green forests and crystal lakes. On the other side of the world, vast colonies of slaves labour in the infamous spice mines. Spice smugglers can make vast profits on the 'Kessel Run.'

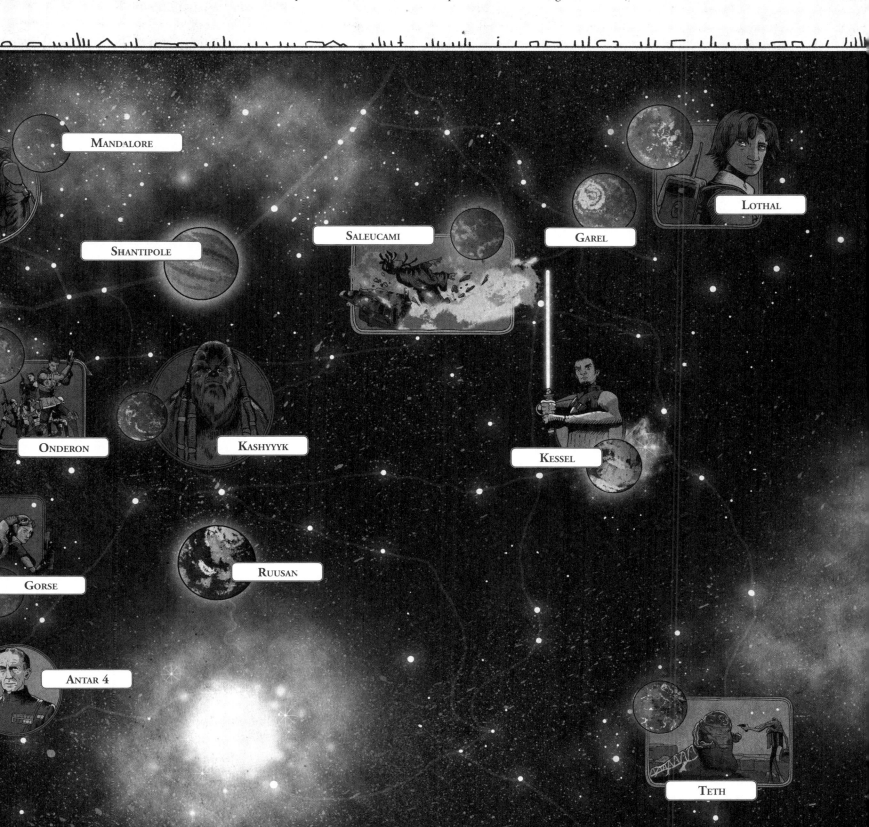

RUUSAN: During the Clone Wars, one of Ruusan's three moons hid a Separatist base, Skytop Station, eavesdropping on Republic transmissions. General Grievous took the captured R2-D2 here to unlock the Republic secrets in his databanks. The astromech was rescued by Anakin Skywalker.

SALEUCAMI: Many people who wished to escape the chaos of the Clone Wars settled on remote Saleucami, including clone trooper Cut Lawquane, who deserted to raise a family. War did, eventually, reach the planet, as the Republic and the Separatists clashed in one of the final battles of the conflict.

SHANTIPOLE: Lightning storms rage among the mountain spires of Shantipole; the atmosphere is highly dangerous for piloting starships. It is here, away from the watchful gaze of the Empire, that the Mon Calamari engineer Quarrie invented the prototype Blade Wing or B-wing fighter for the rebels.

SHILI: The homeworld of the Togruta, who are instantly recognisable thanks to their brightly patterned skin, head-tails, and montrals – hollow, cone-shaped horns which allow the Togruta to track movement. Two famous Jedi hailed from Shili: Jedi Master Shaak Ti and the Padawan Ahsoka Tano.

TETH: A mountainous jungle planet in a Hutt-controlled area of Wild Space. Teth was once inhabited by the bizarre monks of the B'omarr Order, whose brains were transplanted into spider-like droid bodies. It was the scene of the daring rescue of the infant Rotta the Hutt by Anakin Skywalker.

LOTHAL

A once tranquil agricultural world known for its jogan fruit, Lothal suffered under the Galactic Empire, which ruthlessly strip-mined the planet for ores and crystals to fuel military production. It was on Lothal that the rebel cell founded by Kanan Jarrus and Hera Syndulla came together and won a series of notable victories against Imperial forces.

5 BBY: Ezra Bridger, an orphan, lives in an abandoned communications tower. He collects Imperial helmets, including that of a TIE fighter pilot who attacked him.

5 BBY: Ezra Bridger joins the crew of the *Ghost*.

4 BBY: The Lothal rebels occupy a radio tower and broadcast a stirring message of resistance against the Empire.

4 BBY: The Lothal rebels manage to destroy a new prototype TIE fighter, on Empire Day.

5 BBY: Pursued by Kanan Jarrus, Ezra Bridger flees with stolen Imperial cargo.

4 BBY: Darth Vader proves more than a match for Kanan Jarrus and Ezra Bridger.

4 BBY: With the failure of the Grand Inquisitor, the Emperor sends a replacement to Lothal to root out the rebel cell: the Dark Lord of the Sith Darth Vader.

4 BBY: Zeb Orrelios loses at sabacc to the legendary gambler Lando Calrissian.

6 BBY: Zare Leonis and Merei Spanjaf, schoolmates at AppSci, begin to investigate the Empire's activities.

LOTH-CAT

Loth-cats are a feline species native to Lothal. They stalk the grasslands, hunting their main prey the loth-rat.

5 BBY: Ezra Bridger infiltrates the Imperial academy on Lothal, where he meets Zare Leonis – who also has a rebellious hidden agenda..

4 BBY: Hera Syndulla knocks out Senator Gall Trayvis, whom she has discovered is posing as a rebel sympathiser to lure them into a trap.

4 BBY: Kanan Jarrus takes his apprentice Ezra Bridger to the old Jedi Temple on Lothal. Here, Ezra is tested and is able to commune with Master Yoda.

5 BBY: Old Jho's Pit Stop, a cantina in the small settlement of Jhothal, is an outpost friendly to the rebels.

· BBY: Ezra Bridger and Garazeb Orrelios are sent out for fruit but end up stealing a TIE fighter.

14 BBY: Ephraim and Mira Bridger start to make underground radio broadcasts against Imperial rule – the Bridger Transmissions.

STARKILLER BASE

The First Order's ultimate weapon, even more fearsome than the Death Star, is constructed from an entire planet. It fires a beam of phantom energy through hyperspace and is capable of destroying entire star systems. Recharging the weapon requires that the power of a sun be utterly drained.

Now reunited with Rey, Han Solo, Finn and Chewbacca plan to plant explosives to expose the crucial oscillator. With this destroyed, the weapon will overload, blowing up the entire base.

GENERAL HUX

Planetary shields prevent ships from landing – unless they are travelling at lightspeed. Han Solo and Chewbacca bring the *Millennium Falcon* out of hyperspace beneath the shield, an incredibly dangerous and skilful manoeuvre.

Kylo Ren attempts to torture and turn Rey to the dark side. However, she fights back, using the Force instinctively.

Kylo Ren, shot and wounded by Chewbacca, pursues Rey and Finn outside the base. He duels Finn and seriously wounds him, before Rey recovers a lightsaber and attacks furiously. The Knight of Ren is defeated. As the Starkiller weapon is destroyed and the planet begins to crumble, Rey is rescued by Chewbacca in the *Falcon*.

Rey and Finn escape from Starkiller Base in a stolen First Order snowspeeder, pursued by stormtroopers. They are able to fight off their attackers.

General Hux rallies the troops of the First Order as he prepares to fire the Starkiller weapon for the first time. The awesomely powerful beam destroys five key Republic star systems and much of their navy.

With the planetary shield brought down, Poe Dameron's fighter squadrons arrive to attack the oscillator.

Finn, who was once stationed on the base, helps Han Solo and Chewbacca sneak inside. He aims to rescue Rey.

CAPTAIN PHASMA

KYLO REN

Finn, Han Solo and Chewbacca make their way inside and capture Captain Phasma. They force her to lower the base's shields.

Kylo Ren fully embraces the dark side, murdering his father, Han Solo.

Rey escapes from her cell by using a Jedi mind trick and looks for a way off the planet. By chance, she finds Finn, Han Solo and Chewbacca infiltrating the base.

The mysterious Supreme Leader Snoke prefers to talk to his underlings via a giant hologram in his fearsome throne room. It is here that he orders Hux to use the Starkiller Base against the Republic.

22 BBY: A series of attempts are made on the life of Senator Padmé Amidala. Venomous kouhuns are smuggled into her apartment while she sleeps.

19 BBY: Chancellor Palpatine is revealed as the Sith Lord Darth Sidious, and Jedi Masters Mace Windu, Saesee Tiin, Agen Kolar and Kit Fisto attempt to arrest him in his offices. Sidious destroys them.

CORUSCANT

Coruscant's surface is one colossal city, with skytowers reaching thousands of storeys into the sky. It was also the seat of government for the Old Republic and, later, the Galactic Empire. Representatives from thousands of worlds met to argue in the Senate – until the Emperor dissolved it and took absolute power for himself.

After the fall of the Empire, the New Republic's government moved from system to system; fatefully, to the Hosnian system, which was destroyed by the First Order in 34 ABY.

22 BBY: Obi-Wan Kenobi hitches a ride on the assassin's ASN-121 courier droid.

The vast Galactic Senate Building dominates the Senate District. The chamber held 1,024 delegations from the worlds of the Republic.

22 BBY: Anakin Skywalker commandeers a speeder, and the two Jedi chase the assassin through the city.

19 BBY: Anakin Skywalker and Chancellor Palpatine attend the Galaxies Opera House performance of Squid Lake.

22 BBY: The Jedi track Padmé's would-be assassin to the Outlander Club, where a Balosar criminal attempts to sell Obi-Wan death-sticks.

Dexter Jettster runs a diner in the run-down industrial district, CoCo Town.

22 BBY: The assassin, a shape-shifting Clawdite called Zam Wessell, is cornered – but then assassinated by her employer Jango Fett.

19 BBY: Anakin Skywalker falls to the dark side and is dubbed Darth Vader by his new Master, Sidious. For his first task, he leads the clone troopers of the 501st Legion to the Jedi Temple, where they slaughter the Jedi.

32 BBY: The child Anakin Skywalker is brought before the Jedi Council. Despite their misgivings, they agree that he may be trained.

25 BBY: The Jedi Temple has stood for millennia and seen generations of Padawan learners train in the ways of the Force. It endured until the Jedi Purge; afterwards, it became the palace of the Emperor.

22 BBY: Yoda trains younglings in the Jedi Temple. Low-power training lightsabers are provided, to minimise the risk of injury.

21 BBY: The giant and terrifying Zillo Beast, brought to Coruscant from the planet Malastare for research, rampages through the capital.

CAN-CELL

KASHYYYK

A lush forest planet which is home to the mighty Wookiee species. They live in settlements built into the giant wroshyr trees, whose wood is also incorporated into much Wookiee technology. The Wookiees are known for their great physical strength and aptitude for engineering. During the rule of Emperor Palpatine, the species was used as slave labour.

19 BBY: Master Yoda is sent to Kashyyyk with a battalion of clone troopers to reinforce the Wookiees in their battle against Separatist forces.

19 BBY: Separatist troops target the Kashyyyk oil refinery in an attempt to cut off fuel supplies.

The famous *Raddaugh Gnasp* fluttercraft, manufactured by Appazanna Engineering Works, sees action during the Clone Wars.

Oevvaor catamaran-style gunships, built by Appazanna Engineering, are crewed by one pilot and three gunners.

The signature weapon of the Wookiee warrior is the bowcaster.

Kashyyyk is one of several planets where the insects called can-cells can be found.

Wookiees are enslaved by the Empire and sent to work on planets like Kessel. A Wookiee revolt is put down by General Kahdah.

19 BBY: Order 66 is issued, but Master Yoda senses the danger and slays the troopers who try to assassinate him.

19 BBY: Separatist troops rush across the lagoon to the capital city, Karchirho. They are met on the beaches by a Wookiee army and the Republic's clone troops, who manage to repel the enemy.

MANDALORE

A once beautiful world scarred by centuries of war; endless battles have turned it into a vast desert studded with domed cities. The feared Mandalorian warriors were exiled to the moon of Concordia, while the New Mandalorians attempted to rebuild their world in peace. During the Clone Wars, the New Mandalorian ruler Duchess Satine Kryze was overthrown by the terrorist group Death Watch, despite the efforts of her old friend Obi-Wan Kenobi.

MANDALORIAN WARRIORS

Mandalorians are some of the galaxy's most feared warriors. Their distinctive armour contains an arsenal of deadly weapons, and they are skilled in the use of personal rocket packs. The bounty hunters Jango and Boba Fett favoured Mandalorian armour.

DUCHESS SATINE KRYZE

Duchess Satine Kryze leads the New Mandalorian Government.

The Peace Park is a memorial to the victims of Mandalore's violent past.

PEACE PARK

TEE VA

120 BBY: Moogan smugglers, who have been caught selling contaminated tea, shoot it out with Mandalorian security forces as Duchess Satine struggles with corruption.

20 BBY: Cadets Amis, Korkie, Lagos and Soniee discover that Prime Minister Almec is tied to the black market on Mandalore.

19 BBY: Ziton Moj of Darth Maul's Shadow Collective attacks innocent Mandalorians as part of their plan to take over the planet.

Sabine Wren and her friend Ketsu Onyo attend the Imperial Academy together, before deciding to become bounty hunters.

20 BBY: Duchess Satine attempts to escape Death Watch in a speeder but is captured and imprisoned.

19 BBY: Duchess Satine is executed by Darth Maul and dies in Obi-Wan Kenobi's arms.

19 BBY: Darth Maul installs the disgraced former Prime Minister Almec as the puppet leader of Mandalore.

PRIME MINISTER ALMEC

20 BBY: Dr Zak Zaz ponders the poisoning of hundreds of schoolchildren. He discovers it is due to contaminated tea sold by smugglers linked to Prime Minister Almec.

19 BBY: Darth Sidious travels to Mandalore to put an end to Maul's dangerous criminal organisation the Shadow Collective. He defeats both Maul and his brother Savage Opress in an epic duel, executing Savage, but allowing Maul to live.

19 BBY: Pre Vizsla, leader of the Mandalorian terror cell Death Watch, duels Maul using the ancient darksaber, but the Sith Lord destroys him.

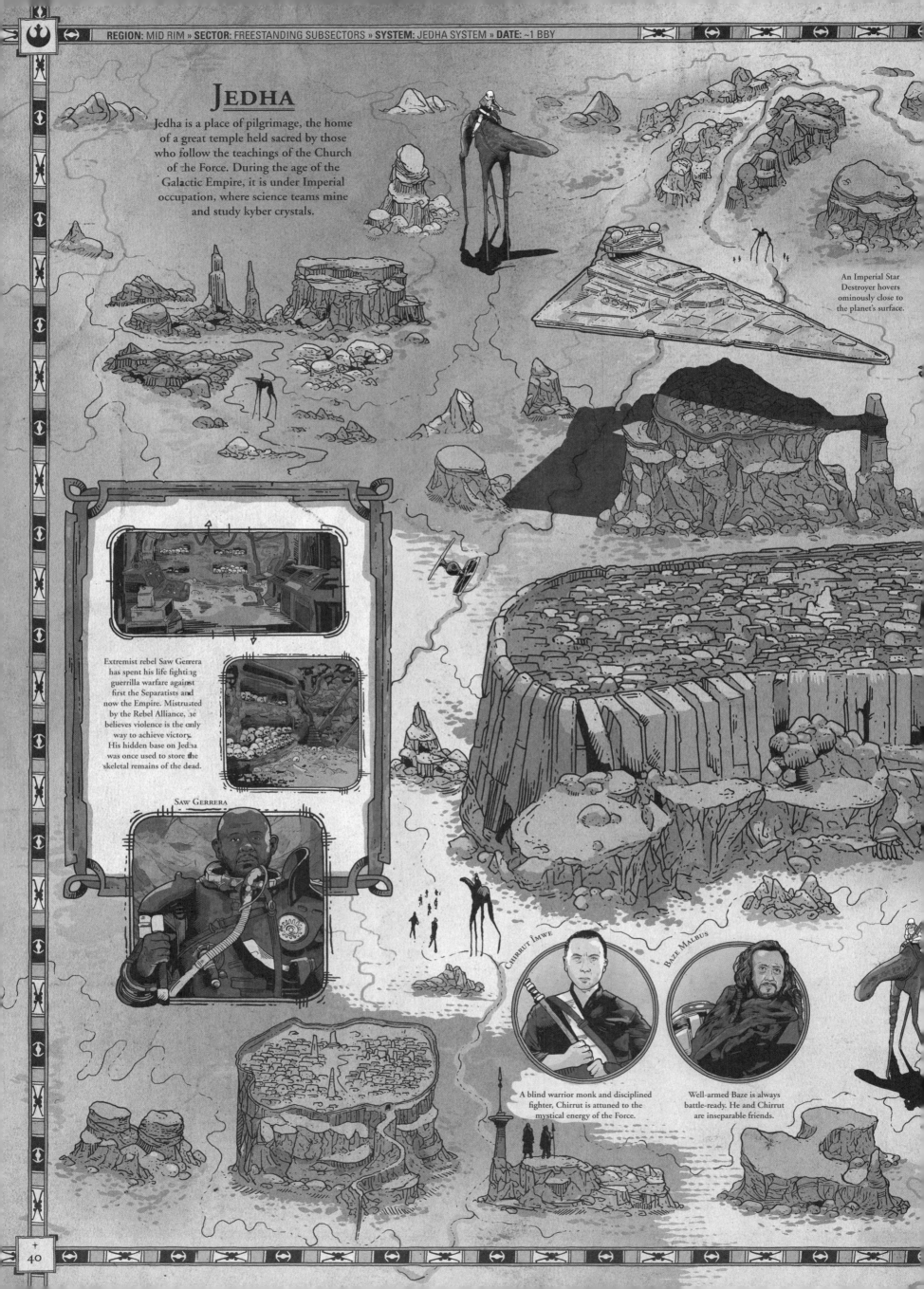

JEDHA

Jedha is a place of pilgrimage, the home of a great temple held sacred by those who follow the teachings of the Church of the Force. During the age of the Galactic Empire, it is under Imperial occupation, where science teams mine and study kyber crystals.

An Imperial Star Destroyer hovers ominously close to the planet's surface.

Extremist rebel Saw Gerrera has spent his life fighting guerrilla warfare against first the Separatists and now the Empire. Mistrusted by the Rebel Alliance, he believes violence is the only way to achieve victory. His hidden base on Jedha was once used to store the skeletal remains of the dead.

SAW GERRERA

CHIRRUT ÎMWE

BAZE MALBUS

A blind warrior monk and disciplined fighter, Chirrut is attuned to the mystical energy of the Force.

Well-armed Baze is always battle-ready. He and Chirrut are inseparable friends.

Saw Gerrera's hideout is hidden beneath this ancient ruin.

TEMPLE OF THE KYBER

The holy city, like many settlements on Jedha, sits atop a natural mesa.

Pilgrims on Jedha can be recognised by their distinctive, often ornate robes.

Stormtroopers patrol the chilly sands of Jedha atop long-legged mounts.

ABEDNEDO TO TATOOINE

ABEDNEDO: Emperor Palpatine's last cruel order, Operation: Cinder was a revenge scheme that was to be put into effect only on his death. It targeted entire worlds for destruction, including Abednedo. An Abednedo pilot, Ello Asty, later flew for the Resistance at Starkiller Base.

BARDOTTA: A frozen, mountainous planet whose people are fascinated by mysticism. During the Clone Wars, Jedi Master Mace Windu and Jar Jar Binks foiled a plot by a sinister cult to drain Bardottan Queen Julia's life energy and channel it into their leader, Mother Talzin.

BOTHAWUI: Dense rings of asteroids around the gas giant Bothawui offer a masterclass for pilots, who must be highly skilled to navigate them. It was the scene of a major space battle during the Clone Wars, in which the tactical genius of Anakin Skywalker was key to defeating General Grievous.

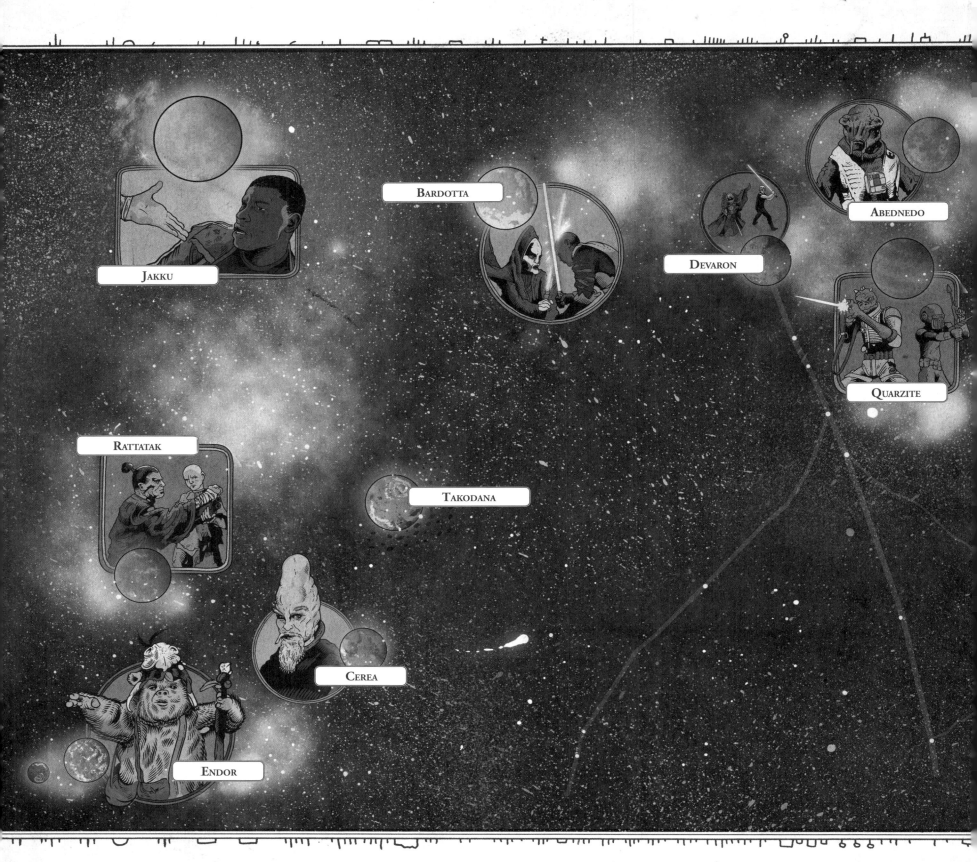

JAKKU

BARDOTTA

DEVARON

ABEDNEDO

QUARZITE

RATTATAK

TAKODANA

CEREA

ENDOR

JAKKU: Jakku is littered with the wreckage of starships that fell from orbit during the last great battle of the Galactic Civil War. Scavengers comb the debris for salvage. One such scavenger, Rey, was abandoned on Jakku as a child, and was later caught up in the struggle between the Resistance and the First Order.

MALASTARE: The homeworld of the Dug species, Malastare is a forest world whose core is rich in valuable fuel. During the Clone Wars, the Republic tested an electro-proton bomb here, designed to knock out droid armies. However, it awakened a colossal Zillo Beast, which then went on a rampage.

NABOO: One of the galaxy's most beautiful worlds, with lush grasslands, winding rivers and tall waterfalls. The crust of the planet is riddled with holes and passages which are filled with water. These can be used as a quick means of submarine travel from one part of the planet to another.

Naboo was the homeworld of the Sith Lord Darth Sidious. Born Sheev Palpatine, his scheming made him first a Senator, then Supreme Chancellor, then Emperor. The Trade Federation's invasion of his home planet was one of the first moves in his grand plan to seize control of the galaxy.

QUARZITE: The surface of Quarzite cannot support life. Its inhabitants the Belugans and the Kage fought a long war for control of the underground crystal caverns. Access to these caverns is only possible using a giant turbolift which leads from an orbiting space station down into the planet's crust.

CEREA: A beautiful world, largely unspoiled by the ravages of technology. It is home to the Cerean people, whose towering cone-shaped skulls contain a binary brain. Ki-Adi-Mundi was a famous Cerean Jedi Master who won many victories during the Clone Wars with his Galactic Marines.

CHRISTOPHSIS: Crystal forests cover the surface of Christophsis, tall jagged spires of turquoise rising from fields of hexagonal 'tiles'. A fierce battle was fought here in the early days of the Clone Wars, in which Generals Kenobi and Skywalker triumphed over the Separatist Whorm Loathsom.

DEVARON: A green and pleasant world of forests, rivers and tropical jungles, inhabited by the Devaronian species. The Jedi Temple on Devaron was attacked during the Clone Wars by the monstrous Savage Opress, who slew Jedi Master Halsey. Later, Luke Skywalker honed his lightsaber skills here.

ENDOR: This small forest moon orbits the gas giant of the same name. It is home to the furry Ewoks, the swamp-dwelling Duloks, and the Yuzzums of the grasslands. Endor was famously the scene of the titanic battle in which the second Death Star was destroyed and Emperor Palpatine perished.

GEONOSIS: An arid world whose insectoid inhabitants were skilled in engineering. The vast factories of Geonosis created millions of battle droids for the Separatists, and the Empire began to construct the first Death Star in orbit. Later, the planet was sterilised, killing almost all life.

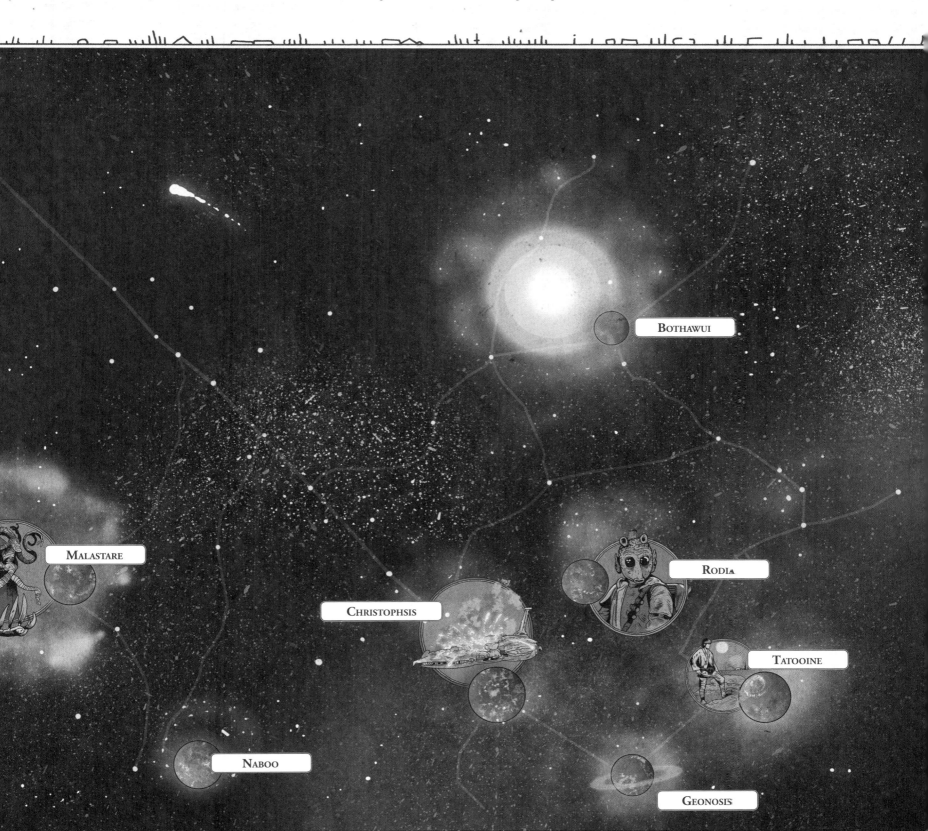

RATTATAK: A dry, rocky world plagued by the attacks of pirates and warlords. One such pirate, Hal'Sted, owned a slave – the young Asajj Ventress. When Hal'Sted was killed on Rattatak, the Jedi Ky Narec took in Ventress and began to train her. His death at the hands of pirates led to her fall to the dark side.

RODIA: A warm, damp planet of swamps and jungles, Rodia is the homeworld of the Rodian species. During the Clone Wars, Rodia wavered between supporting the Republic and supporting the Separatists, but eventually Senator Padmé Amidala helped to sway them to the Republic's cause.

TAKODANA: Situated halfway between the Core Worlds and the wild frontier, Takodana is a popular stop for travellers, explorers, fugitives and smugglers. The famous pirate Maz Kanata owned a castle here, where strange beings from all over the galaxy gathered to relax or do business.

TATOOINE: What little moisture there is on dusty Tatooine has to be extracted from the air by vaporators and is crucial to the survival of life. Humans and others scratch out a living here alongside the native Tusken Raiders – also known as the Sand People – and the Jawas who scavenge the sands.

A largely lawless world, Tatooine is controlled by the Hutt clans and is a hub of criminal activity. Smugglers and bounty hunters flock to shady dives in ports like Mos Eisley, while gamblers bet on deadly podraces and back-room sabacc games in Mos Espa and elsewhere.

34 ABY: Daring Resistance pilot Poe Dameron meets with the explorer Lor San Tekka on Jakku.

TUANUL

34 ABY: The sacred village of Tuanul is populated by members of the Church of the Force.

34 ABY: First Order troops led by Kylo Ren and Captain Phasma destroy Tuanul village and execute all who live there.

34 ABY: BB-8, entrusted with secret information by Poe Dameron, flees the village's destruction.

5 ABY: The Battle of Jakku leaves the surface of the planet littered with debris, and the starship graveyard is formed.

34 ABY: With First Order TIE fighters in pursuit, Finn and Rey escape Jakku in an old YT-1300 freighter.

JAKKU

The desolate planet Jakku was the scene of the last great battle between the Galactic Empire and the Rebel Alliance, a year after the death of the Emperor. The Graveyard of Giants – a vast plain of crashed starships – attracted scavengers, who sold their salvaged technology to local traders.
Few people come to Jakku by choice.

MILLENNIUM FALCON

5 ABY: A capital ship crashes into the planet, fusing the sand into glass and burying itself deep under the surface – the Spike in the Crackle.

KELVIN RAVINE

GRAVEYARD OF GIANTS

34 ABY: The Sitter keeps a lonely vigil on this tower in the shadow of Carbon Ridge. The Teedos sometimes bring him offerings.

PILGRIM'S ROAD

THE SITTER

34 ABY: Rey salvages components, which she will trade for a little food, from the wreck of a Star Destroyer.

34 ABY: Rey's background is shrouded in mystery. She scrapes a living as a scavenger while she awaits her family's return.

TEEDO

SINKING FIELDS

CRATERTOWN

Cratertown is one of Jakku's older settlements. Scavenging is a major industry, as is kesium gas mining.

34 ABY: Old Meru's is a stop along the Pilgrim's Road, where shade and a trough for happabores can be found.

34 ABY: A stolen TIE fighter piloted by Poe Dameron crashes in the Sinking Fields. His passenger, Finn, escapes the wreck.

OLD MERU'S

The Goazon Badlands extend from Carbon Ridge to the Sinking Fields, and from Kelvin Ravine to Niima Outpost.

34 ABY: A Teedo and his luggabeast find and capture BB-8 for salvage.

LUGGABEAST

34 ABY: Finn makes his way through the desert to Niima Outpost.

34 ABY: The scavenger Rey lives in the wreck of this Imperial AT-AT. It is here that she rescues BB-8 from the Teedo.

34 ABY: Bobbajo the Crittermonger deals in animals. He claims his creatures were responsible for the destruction of the first Death Star, but few believe him.

REY'S SPEEDER

34 ABY: The First Order tracks Finn and BB-8 to Niima Outpost, and their TIE fighters attack.

BOBBAJO

CONSTABLE ZUVIO

34 ABY: Niima Outpost, named after the Hutt outlaw who founded it, is a trading post for Jakku's scavengers. Constable Zuvio keeps the peace.

NIIMA OUTPOST

UNKAR PLUTT

34 ABY: Unkar Plutt, known as 'the Blobfish', is the junkboss at Niima Outpost. His prices are unfair, but his customers have no choice.

General Solo's strike team arrives on the Endor moon in a stolen Imperial shuttle, the *Tydirium*.

Luke Skywalker meets his father, Darth Vader, and begs him to return to the light. Vader refuses and takes his son to the Death Star to meet his Master, the Emperor.

ENDOR

This small forest moon, orbiting the planet Endor, was just another remote galactic backwater until the end of the Galactic Civil War, when it was the scene of a decisive battle. The Ewoks of the Endor Moon, while short in stature, proved invaluable allies. They caused havoc while the second Death Star's shield generator was assaulted by the commando team led by General Solo.

An energy shield, protecting the unfinished Death Star, is projected from the moon's surface.

The rebel strike team engages an Imperial scout trooper patrol.

With the help of the Ewoks, Chewbacca captures an Imperial AT-ST walker.

Imperial scout troopers and AT-STs are deployed on the Endor moon, anticipating a rebel attack.

Rebel commandos are the responsibility of General Madine, a veteran guerilla fighter.

The Empire sets up an ambush on the Sanctuary Moon.

Yuzzums, like the singer Joh Yowza, are native to Endor.

Ewoks capture the strike team but mistake C-3PO for a god. The droid persuades them to release his friends.

BRIGHT TREE VILLAGE

Chief of the Ewok village is Chirpa, while the shaman is Logray.

Ewoks use guerrilla tactics and cunning traps to stun the Imperial forces.

The rebels join forces with the Ewoks and plan a raid on the shield generator.

The mountains of Endor are home to the giant Gorax species.

The Emperor reveals that the rebels have stepped into his trap: the battle station is fully operational. It fires on the Mon Calamari star cruiser *Liberty*, destroying it.

EMPEROR PALPATINE

BATTLE OF ENDOR

The second Death Star is even larger and more powerful than the first, and the rebels plan an all-out raid to destroy it before it becomes operational. However, they are being lured into a trap, designed to end the Galactic Civil War in the Empire's favour. As General Solo's commando team tries to take down the station's protective shield, a battle rages in orbit...

CRIX MADINE

HORTON SALM

SILA KOTT

ADMIRAL ACKBAR

WEDGE ANTILLES

LANDO CALRISSIAN

GENERAL CRACKEN

NIEN NUNB

General Calrissian pilots the *Millennium Falcon*. When it is revealed that the Death Star is operational, he orders Gold Squadron to engage the Star Destroyer *Executor*, to draw fire away from the rebel cruisers.

Luke Skywalker and Darth Vader duel as the Emperor tries to turn the young Jedi to the dark side. Skywalker strikes his father down but then refuses to kill him, surrendering.

As the Emperor prepares to kill Luke Skywalker, the goodness in Anakin Skywalker is awakened. He casts his Master down at the cost of his own life.

Shara Bey

Grizz Frix

Moff Tiaan Jerjerrod

The *Millennium Falcon*, piloted by Lando Calrissian and Nien Nunb, and Wedge Antilles' X-wing fly into the superstructure of the Death Star and destroy the main reactor.

. Admiral Piett commands the flagship *Executor*. It is destroyed when A-wing pilot Arvel Crynyd crashes into the bridge, and the ship in turn crashes into the Death Star.

Admiral Piett

Admiral Rae Sloane

RODIA

A hot, humid world covered in rainforests and swamps.
The Rodians live in floating cities contained within vast
environmental domes, which protect the inhabitants
from the more extreme effects of the climate.

22 BBY: Padmé
Amidala arrives on
Rodia to persuade
Senator Onaconda
Farr to stay loyal
to the Republic.

22 BBY: More
by luck than
judgement, Jar Jar
Binks escapes the
battle droids which
are trying to
kill him.

22 BBY: Senator
Farr reveals he has
already pledged
allegiance to the
Separatists and
takes Amidala into
custody.

22 BBY: Battle
droids ambush
Jar Jar Binks
and C-3PO

22 BBY: Amidala
is imprisoned in a
high-security tower
while battle droids
hunt for Jar Jar
Binks and C-3PO.

22 BBY: Trade
Federation Viceroy
Nute Gunray arrives
on Rodia to capture
Senator Amidala.

22 BBY:
C-3PO is
captured by
battle droids.

22 BBY: The lurking
'Boogie Monster' – a
Kwazel Maw – comes
to Jar Jar's rescue.

22 BBY: Senator Amidala makes
a daring escape from prison,
exploiting poor battle-droid logic.

22 BBY: Jar Jar
Binks is mistaken
for a Jedi by the
Separatists and
tries to rescue
Amidala.

22 BBY: C-3PO
manages to send a
distress call about
Senator Amidala's
capture.

21 BBY: Posing as a Jedi, the bounty hunter Cad Bane takes a Force-sensitive Rodian child away on the orders of Senator Palpatine, who plots to use his powers for evil.

The swamps of Rodia are home to countless varieties of snake.

GHEST

Ghests are deadly, snake-like predators that can bite a humanoid in half. Luke Skywalker slew one near the tomb of the Jedi Huulik.

GEONOSIS

A rocky desert world inhabited by an insectoid race, whose great domes and spires resemble natural formations. Geonosis was long renowned for its manufacturing industries; the Separatist droid armies were built here, and the first Death Star was partially constructed in orbit. Later, however, the Empire ruthlessly sterilised the planet.

Clone troopers arrive in gunships known as Low Altitude Assault Transports.

LOW ALTITUDE TROOP TRANSPORT

QUEEN KARINA

0 ABY: Darth Vader and the archaeologist Dr Aphra confront the Geonosian Queen on a planet now scoured of life by the Empire.

0 ABY: Assassin droids 0-0-0 and BT-1 make short work of the Queen's battle droids.

21 BBY: Anakin Skywalker and Luminara Unduli arrive on Geonosis, charged with capturing the planet for the Republic.

21 BBY: Queen Karina captures Jedi Master Luminara Unduli and enslaves her using a brain worm.

LUMINARA UNDULI

GEONOSIAN

THE SECOND BATTLE OF GEONOSIS

21 BBY: Despite heavy losses, the Republic forces prevail. The Geonosian droid factory is destroyed – a heavy blow to the Separatist war effort.

21 BBY: The Geonosian Queen, Karina the Great, rules over the Geonosians and has learned to control the minds of others using vile brain worms.

21 BBY: Padawans Ahsoka Tano and Barriss Offee undertake a daring mission to sabotage a droid factory, while their Masters Skywalker and Unduli distract the enemy.

22 BBY: Obi-Wan contacts the Jedi Council to warn them about Dooku's plot.

22 BBY: Countless battle droids are forged in Geonosis's vast automated factories.

The Empire later harnessed the engineering prowess of the Geonosians, who helped construct the Death Star.

22 BBY: Count Dooku meets with Separatist leaders including the Trade Federation, Banking Clan and Techno Union.

22 BBY: In a factory mishap, C-3PO's head is accidentally attached to a battle droid's body.

22 BBY: Mace Windu slays Jango Fett while his clone-son Boba watches in horror.

22 BBY: Obi-Wan, Anakin and Padmé are captured and chained in the arena, where giant beasts attack them.

22 BBY: Mace Windu leads the Jedi into battle – but they are outnumbered and surrounded by battle droids.

22 BBY: With his forces decimated by the Jedi's new clone troopers, Dooku flees to a secret hangar where his Solar Sailer awaits.

22 BBY: Count Dooku defeats Obi-Wan and Anakin in battle, but then Master Yoda intervenes and duels his old apprentice.

Brain worms can turn sentient beings into mind-controlled zombies.

BRAIN WORM

Geonosians live in vast hive-spires.

TATOOINE

Once described as the place that's furthest away from the bright centre of the universe, the remote desert planet Tatooine bakes beneath its twin suns. It is home to two native species, Jawas and Tuskens, as well as a wide variety of newcomers. Tatooine is famous as the homeworld of two great Jedi – Anakin and Luke Skywalker.

MOS ESPA

A port city run by the Hutt Clan, Mos Espa is known for its dangerous podracing circuit and especially the famous Boonta Eve Classic Podrace.

32 BBY: Junk dealer Watto, a Toydarian, makes a bet with Qui-Gon Jinn on a podrace. The stakes are a new hyperdrive for Queen Amidala's ship and the freedom of the slave boy Anakin Skywalker.

PIT DROID

19 BBY: Following the Jedi Purge, Obi-Wan Kenobi brought the infant Luke Skywalker to Tatooine. He would watch over the child for the next 19 years.

OLD BEN KENOBI

0 BBY: Luke Skywalker, out searching for R2-D2, is menaced by a gang of Sand People but rescued at the last moment by Obi-Wan Kenobi.

WOMP RAT

Banthas are used by the Sand People as mounts and beasts of burden.

Dewbacks are large reptilian beasts, so named because they drink the morning dew which condenses on their backs.

DEWBACK

JAWAS

R2-D2

0 BBY: Separated from each other, R2-D2 and C-3PO are both captured by Jawa scavengers.

0 BBY: The escape pod launched from the *Tantive IV* blockade runner crashes in the desert. Its occupants, the droids R2-D2 and C-3PO, set off in search of help, while Imperial troops track them.

"LOOK SIR, DROIDS."

JABBA'S PALACE

Jabba the Hutt's palace on Tatooine was once the site of a monastery run by the B'omarr Order.

WORRT

Worrts are large warty predators who conceal themselves in the desert sands to await unwary prey.

EOPIE

32 BBY: Darth Maul tracks Qui-Gon Jinn, his Padawan Obi-Wan, and Queen Amidala to Tatooine, where he clashes with the Jedi Master.

NABOO ROYAL STARSHIP

Sand people travel single-file, to hide their numbers.

BANTHAS

22 BBY: When his mother Shmi dies at the hands of the Sand People, Anakin Skywalker gives in to his anger and slaughters the tribe.

THE GREAT PIT OF CARKOON

GONK DROID

4 ABY: The Great Pit of Carkoon contains a terrible sarlacc and was a favourite site for Jabba to dispose of his enemies. Luke Skywalker destroyed his sail barge here.

RONTO

Rontos are popular mounts among Jawas.

MOS EISLEY

TUSKEN RAIDERS

Mos Eisley spaceport, once described as a 'wretched hive of scum and villainy.'

Luke Skywalker learned to fly on Tatooine, piloting a T-16 Skyhopper.

T-16

A small outpost outside the town of Anchorhead, and a meeting place for local farmers.

The moisture farm owned by Owen and Beru Lars, where Luke Skywalker grew up.

TOSCHE STATION

CHRISTOPHSIS

Christophsis is known for its crystal landscape, with vast plains of hexagonal gems and jagged forests of spires. It was the site of a desperate battle during the Clone Wars, in which Republic forces under General Kenobi and General Skywalker defeated a Separatist invasion force.

Anakin Skywalker gets an unwelcome surprise as he is introduced to his new Padawan apprentice, Ahsoka Tano.

Clone troopers of the 501st Legion fight a desperate battle against the Separatist battle droids.

Clone troopers set up powerful artillery positions to beat back the Separatist advance.

Republic commandos ambush the battle droids from zip-lines.

Captain Rex is the first to spot the Separatist's energy shield. His squad, Torrent Company, takes heavy casualties skirmishing with the battle droids.

The Jedi Kenobi, Skywalker and Tano, along with Clone Captain Rex and R2-D2, discuss battle tactics.

ARMOURED ASSAULT TANK

The Separatist forces are protected by an energy shield that moves as they advance, leading the Jedi Anakin Skywalker and Ahsoka Tano to mount a stealth raid.

A traitorous clone trooper, Slick, is found to be passing information to the Separatists. Commander Cody knocks him out.

LR-57 combat droids protect the Separatist shield generators, but the Jedi nevertheless destroy them.

Anakin Skywalker destroys the Separatists' Octuptarra combat tri-droids.

Battle droids advance on the clone trooper positions in seemingly endless waves.

Separatist forces on Christophsis are led by the Kerkoiden, General Whorm Loathsom.

GENERAL WHORM LOATHSOM

Obi-Wan Kenobi stalls for time as Anakin and Ahsoka assault the Separatist shield generator. His scheming pays off, and the Republic are victorious.

NABOO

A small but beautiful jewel of a world, Naboo was the home planet of Queen Padmé Amidala and Senator Sheev Palpatine – who would go on to rule the galaxy as Emperor. Naboo is inhabited by the human society of the same name, and the native Gungans, an amphibious race who live in underwater cities.

THEED

The beautiful city of Theed is the capital of the Naboo. Vast waterfalls cascade over the cliffs on which it perches. Beneath the Royal Palace is a hangar and a generator complex.

32 BBY: The Royal Palace is captured by the Trade Federation's forces, who have occupied the city. They hope to force Queen Amidala to sign a treaty surrendering to them. She escapes with the help of the Jedi, and along with her loyal troops they launch a raid to retake the city.

CAPTAIN PANAKA

The young Anakin Skywalker accidentally steals a Naboo Starfighter and pilots it into orbit.

HANGAR

GENERATOR COMPLEX

The sinister Sith Lord Darth Maul strikes down Qui-Gon Jinn in the palace's generator complex.

Obi-Wan Kenobi avenges the death of his Master by defeating Darth Maul. The assassin is cut in two and falls into the depths of the facility.

32 BBY: Naboo is ruled by an elected King or Queen. At the time of the invasion, the Queen was Padmé Amidala, who served two terms.

20 BBY: Bounty hunter Cad Bane kidnaps Chancellor Palpatine during the Festival of Light, but the plot is thwarted by an undercover Obi-Wan Kenobi.

LAKE PAONGA

Gungan warriors ride kaadus into battle, and are armed with atlatls – long, flexible wooden poles which can sling explosives up to 30 metres.

22 BBY: Jedi Knight Anakin Skywalker is secretly married to Padmé Amidala.

21 BBY: The insane Doctor Nuvo Vindi, working for the Separatists, engineers the deadly Blue Shadow Virus in his secret laboratory.

NUVO VINDI

Docile, plant-eating shaaks are bred for food and sometimes used as pack animals.

SHAAK

GUNGAN WARRIOR

32 BBY: The Battle of Naboo is fought between the Gungans and the Trade Federation's battle droids. All seems lost until the droid control ship is destroyed in orbit by Anakin Skywalker.

LIANORM SWAMP

Predatory tusk-cats are found on Naboo and can even be used as mounts.

TUSK-CAT

The Gungan Sacred Place is an ancient monument, important to the Gungans, north of the Lianorm Swamp. A treaty with the Naboo was signed here.

BATTLE OF NABOO

32 BBY: Jedi Master Qui-Gon Jinn and his Padawan Obi-Wan Kenobi escape the Trade Federation and land on Naboo to warn the Queen. They meet a Gungan outcast, Jar Jar Binks.

PLANET CORE

Naboo's crust is porous and full of water. A bongo submarine can travel great distances beneath the surface, if it does not fall foul of giant sea-beasts such as the colo claw fish, opee and sando.

32 BBY: The Gungans are ruled by a High Council, chaired by a Boss. At the time of the invasion, Boss Nass is in charge.

The city of Otoh Gunga is the underwater capital city of the Gungans. The tough bubbles that it is made from are grown by the Gungans from the planet's natural plasma.

OTOH GUNGA

COLO CLAW FISH

ANDELM IV TO UTAPAU

ANDELM IV: A remote world noted for its beetles, a source of the rare mineral dedlanite. During the Galactic Civil War a crime lord called Jaum enslaved the population, forcing them to harvest dedlanite for the Empire. His plans were foiled by the Wookiee Chewbacca and his friend Zarro.

ARKANIS: Rain falls endlessly on gloomy Arkanis, ranging from drizzle to thunderstorms. The Empire built an academy here, run by Commandant Brendol Hux, to train a generation of elite officers. It was also the site of Project Harvester, which brought Force-sensitive children here for mysterious purposes.

BESPIN: A gas giant with no land, just layers of dense gas through which strange creatures swim. Valuable tibanna gas is collected from vast creatures called beldons and processed in the floating habitats in the upper, breathable layer of atmosphere, including the famous Cloud City.

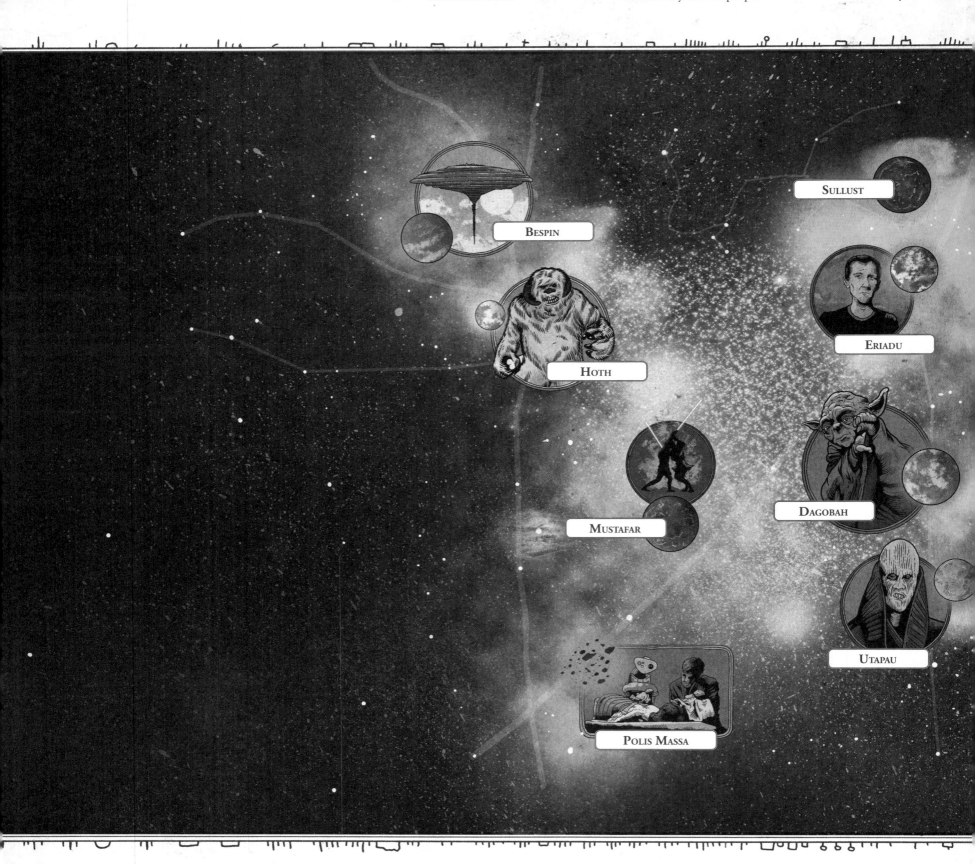

KAMINO: This world is not on any maps. As part of an elaborate plot by Darth Sidious, it was erased from the Jedi Archives, and only rediscovered when Obi-Wan Kenobi was investigating the attempted assassination of the Naboo Senator Padmé Amidala. Kenobi traced the would-be assassin to the Wild Space planet Kamino, an endless ocean whose inhabitants had mastered the science of cloning. The Kaminoans had been paid to create a clone army for the Republic, using the DNA of the bounty hunter Jango Fett – the very assassin Kenobi was chasing.

MUSTAFAR: Lava belches from the volcanoes that cover Mustafar's surface, while swarms of droids harvest rare minerals from the molten rock. Despite the searing heat of this harsh world, it is inhabited by the native Mustafarians, who labour in the mines and factories and live in underground caverns hollowed out by rock-eating lava fleas.

Many dark deeds have taken place on Mustafar. Darth Vader betrayed and slew the Separatist Council here, ending the Clone Wars. He was then defeated and horribly maimed by Obi-Wan Kenobi.

POLIS MASSA: Once a planet, Polis Massa was mysteriously shattered into an asteroid field. A scientific base here studies the disaster, and following Order 66 Yoda and Obi-Wan Kenobi found safety at the research station. It was here that Luke Skywalker and Leia Organa were born.

DAGOBAH: Grand Master Yoda once described Dagobah as 'one of the purest places in the galaxy'. He first came here towards the end of the Clone Wars, drawn by a strange message from his old friend Qui-Gon Jinn, who had died many years earlier. Jinn had discovered the secret of maintaining his identity after death and set Yoda on the path to discover it for himself.

Following his failure to defeat Emperor Palpatine, Yoda exiled himself to Dagobah to meditate on the Force until a new hope could arise. It was here that he met Luke Skywalker.

D'QAR: An obscure, tree-covered planet with no intelligent life and far from the main space lanes, D'Qar is of little interest. This made it a perfect choice as a secret base for the Rebel Alliance and later the Resistance – making it a target for the First Order's Starkiller weapon.

ERIADU: A once-savage wilderness of a world, until colonists tamed it. Among the early pioneers were the Tarkin family, who formed their own militia to protect against pirates and the local wildlife. Wilhuff Tarkin grew up here and learned many harsh lessons in survival.

HOTH: The frozen world Hoth was chosen as the new headquarters of the Rebel Alliance following the Battle of Yavin. The base was discovered by an Imperial probe droid, and Darth Vader moved swiftly to invade the planet. The rebels only narrowly escaped the Echo Base's destruction.

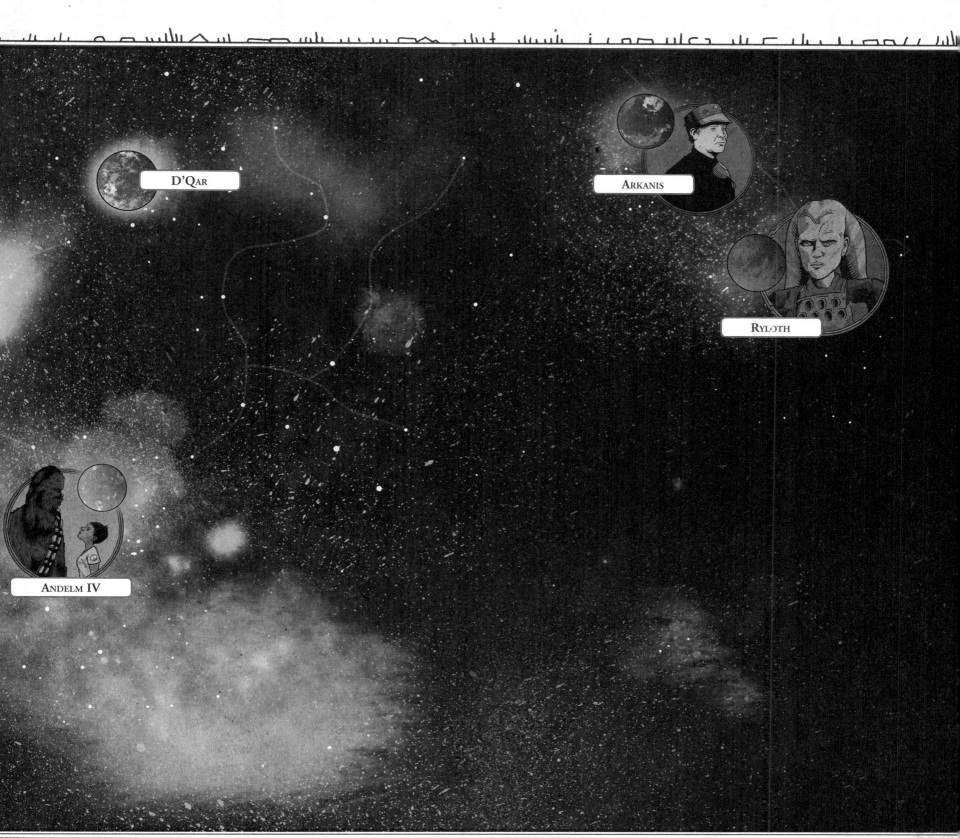

D'QAR

ARKANIS

RYLOTH

ANDELM IV

RYLOTH: Ryloth has seen more than its share of war. During the Clone Wars, it was a battleground between the Republic and the Separatists, as Mace Windu and his forces battled to liberate the planet. Later, freedom fighter Cham Syndulla opposed the Empire's cruel occupation.

A plot by Syndulla and his Free Ryloth group led to Emperor Palpatine and Darth Vader crash-landing on the planet after the Star Destroyer they were travelling in, the *Perilous*, was sabotaged and destroyed. However, the Lords of the Sith were able to escape the assassination attempt.

SULLUST: A barren world of volcanoes and lakes whose people live in vast underground cities. Half of all Sullustans work for the SoroSuub technology corporation. Sullustans are well known as pilots: Nien Nunb famously co-piloted the *Millennium Falcon* at the battle of Endor.

UTAPAU: Hyperwind storms batter the surface of Utapau, forcing many of the planet's inhabitants – the Utai and Pau'ans – to live in the giant sink-holes that lead down into the planet's crust. The Amani, recent settlers on Utapau, are hardy enough to dwell above ground in the grasslands.

During the Clone Wars, Utapau was an important base for the Separatists, and it was here that Obi-Wan Kenobi tracked down General Grievous and challenged him to a duel. After a fierce battle, the Jedi Master managed to tear open the cyborg's armour and destroy him using his own blaster.

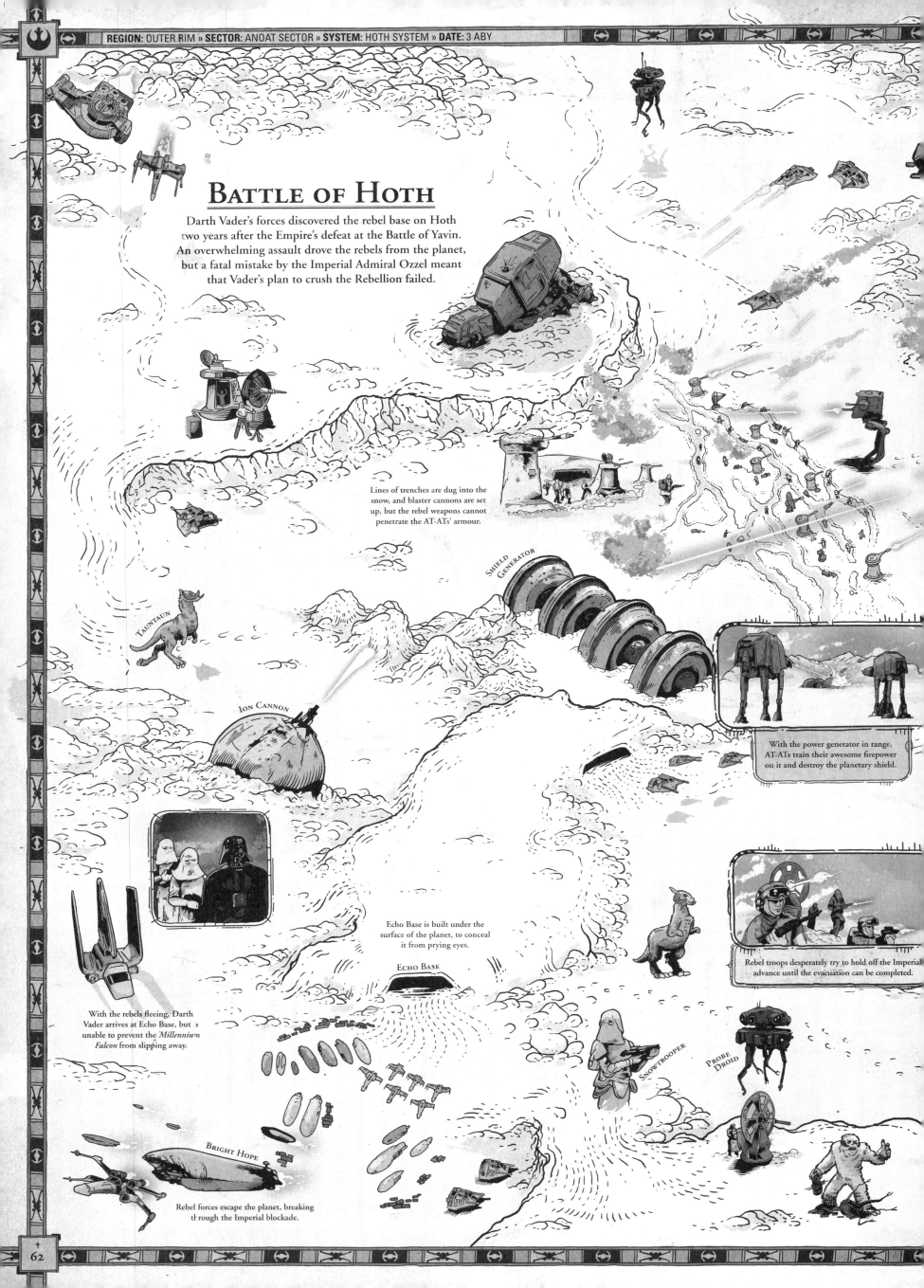

BATTLE OF HOTH

Darth Vader's forces discovered the rebel base on Hoth two years after the Empire's defeat at the Battle of Yavin. An overwhelming assault drove the rebels from the planet, but a fatal mistake by the Imperial Admiral Ozzel meant that Vader's plan to crush the Rebellion failed.

Lines of trenches are dug into the snow, and blaster cannons are set up, but the rebel weapons cannot penetrate the AT-ATs' armour.

SHIELD GENERATOR

TAUNTAUN

ION CANNON

With the power generator in range, AT-ATs train their awesome firepower on it and destroy the planetary shield.

Echo Base is built under the surface of the planet, to conceal it from prying eyes.

ECHO BASE

Rebel troops desperately try to hold off the Imperial advance until the evacuation can be completed.

With the rebels fleeing, Darth Vader arrives at Echo Base, but is unable to prevent the *Millennium Falcon* from slipping away.

SNOWTROOPER

PROBE DROID

BRIGHT HOPE

Rebel forces escape the planet, breaking through the Imperial blockade.

Once an Imperial pilot, Thane Kyrell now flies for the rebels – and must fight against his lover Ciena Ree.

AT-AT

AT-ST

Imperial snowtroopers wear specialised cold-weather gear to protect them in icy conditions.

Wedge Antilles uses the tow-cable on his snowspeeder to entangle an AT-AT's legs, bringing it crashing to the ground.

WAMPA

On patrol, Luke Skywalker is ambushed by a vicious wampa and awakens in the beast's larder.

Having escaped the wampa's cave, Luke is visited by the spirit of Obi-Wan Kenobi, who tells him to go to the Dagobah system. Luke is then rescued by his friend Han Solo.

BLURRG

Twi'lek society is organised into clans, with each clan having its own settlement.

21 BBY: LAAT/I gunships and Acclamator assault ships fly towards Nabat as Republic troops begin their campaign to liberate the planet.

AT-RT

RYLOTH

The homeworld of the Twi'lek species, Ryloth is a warm world with many volcanoes, jungles and valleys. The planet was the scene of decades of fierce resistance by guerrilla fighters, first against the invading Separatists, and then against the Galactic Empire.

22 BBY: Jedi Master Ima-Gun Di makes a heroic last stand against Separatist forces sacrificing his life to secure vital supplies

The most fearsome of all beasts on Ryloth – the terrifying lylek.

LYLEK

JIXUAN DESERT

21 BBY: Mace Windu's liberating forces advance on the capital.

12 BBY: Cham Syndulla's daughter Hera, an ace pilot, leaves Ryloth to fight the Empire.

22 BBY: Twi'lek rebel Cham Syndulla is a key figure in the Ryloth resistance, helping to liberate the planet from the Separatists. Later his rebel cell comes close to destroying the Emperor and Darth Vader.

22 BBY: Separatist general Wat Tambor surrenders to Republic forces commanded by Mace Windu as the planet is liberated.

DRUA'S VILLAGE

14 BBY: Twi'lek rebels sabotage a ship carrying Emperor Palpatine and Darth Vader, and the Sith Lords crash-land on Ryloth. They destroy a Twi'lek village to cover their tracks.

Gutkurrs are deadly predators, part reptile and part insect. The Separatists unleashed them against clone troops outside Nabat.

GUTKURR

21 BBY: Obi-Wan Kenobi is rescued twice, during the Battle of Kamino, by aiwhas.

The vast cloning factories of Kamino could create whole armies of soldiers in a relatively short time.

KAMINO

This remote ocean planet is home to the Kaminoans, a race that has mastered the technology of cloning. Here the Grand Army of the Republic was created from the DNA of bounty hunter Jango Fett. The planet was deleted from the Jedi Archives by the renegade Count Dooku to conceal the secret cloning project and only rediscovered in 22 BBY by Obi-Wan Kenobi.

At the time of the Clone Wars, the Prime Minister of Kamino was Lama Su.

21 BBY: Asajj Ventress attempts to steal the genetic material used to create the clones but is fought off by Anakin Skywalker.

WOLFFE	DOGMA	FIVES	ECHO	CODY	REX
Leader of the clone squad known as the Wolf Pack, under Jedi Master Plo Koon. Survived the Clone Wars and later befriended the rebels.	Member of the elite 501st Legion. Dogma is notable as the trooper who executed traitorous Jedi General Pong Krell in 21 BBY.	Heroic elite ARC trooper who discovered Palpatine's plans to destroy the Jedi – but was framed and killed before he could reveal the truth.	An ARC trooper and member of the 501st, decorated several times for bravery. Seemingly killed during the rescue of Jedi Master Even Piell.	As a Clone Marshal, Cody commanded the 7th Sky Corps. Worked closely with Jedi Master Kenobi, until he attempted to kill him during Order 66.	Loyal, brave ARC trooper who often fought alongside Anakin Skywalker in the 501st. Later befriended the rebellion.

AIWHA

The majestic aiwhas – or air whales – are native to Kamino. These peaceful creatures may be used as mounts.

21 BBY: Separatist aqua droids are deadly enemies on water-worlds like Kamino. Jedi Master Shaak Ti, however, makes short work of them.

22 BBY: Obi-Wan Kenobi confronts Jango Fett, who is behind the assassination attempts on Padmé Amidala. The bounty hunter escapes.

TIPOCA CITY

22 BBY: Obi-Wan Kenobi meets Jango Fett and his clone-son, Boba. He is suspicious of the Mandalorian warrior from the start.

21 BBY: General Grievous leads a Separatist assault or Kamino, hoping to destroy the Republic's supply of clone troops.

HARDCASE

Reckless but deadly with his rotator cannon, Hardcase feared nothing. Sacrificed his life to save his squad during the Battle of Umbara.

WAXER

A member of Ghost Company, Waxer helped liberate Ryloth and Geonosis. Killed as a result of Pong Krell's treachery on Umbara.

TUP

All clones had bio-chips in their brain: to make them follow Order 66; Tup's activated early, causing him to kill a Jedi. He died on Kamino.

JESSE

ARC Trooper and 501st Legion member. Jesse served on Saleucami, Umbara, Ringo Vinda and Anaxes, under Anakin Skywalker.

HEVY

A heavy-weapons expert, Hevy was stationed on the Rishi moon listening post when Separatists attacked. He sacrificed himself to warn the Republic.

99

99, a failed clone of Jango Fett, worked on the janitorial staff of the Kamino training facility. He was wise and beloved by his clone-brothers.

19 BBY: Guided by the voice of Qui-Gon Jinn, Yoda travels to Dagobah, where his old friend appears to him in the form of a swarm of fireflies

Giant omnivorous slugs lurk in the swamps of Dagobah.

SWAMP SLUG

ACCIPIPTERG

The huge, tusked elephoth is native to Dagobah, where it blends in with the environment thanks to its mossy hide.

ELEPHOTH

DAGOBAH

A remote swamp world, teeming with life. Dagobah was the planet chosen by the Jedi Master Yoda when he exiled himself following the triumph of Emperor Palpatine, and where Luke Skywalker trained in the ways of the Jedi. A cave on the planet strong with the dark side of the Force provided a test of his wisdom.

The jubba bird makes its nest from mud and is known for its soothing song.

JUBBA BIRD

Dragonsnakes are stealthy predators which live in the muddy waters of Dagobah, among other planets. A dragonsnake attempted to devour R2-D2 but had to spit him out.

DRAGONSNAKE

MARSH SPIDER

Spiders stalk the swamps, preying on the unwary.

DOMAIN OF EVIL

3 ABY: Luke Skywalker is tested by Yoda, and enters a cave that is strong with the dark side. Though he is told he will not need his weapons, he strikes down a vision of Darth Vader with his lightsaber – only to discover his own face behind the mask.

4 BBY: Yoda mentally communes with Kanan Jarrus and Ezra Bridger.

3 ABY: Luke Skywalker arrives on Dagobah looking for Master Yoda. He fails to recognise the legendary Jedi at first...

3 ABY: Yoda begins to train Luke Skywalker. "A Jedi uses the Force for knowledge and defence, never attack."

3 ABY: Yoda raises Luke's X-wing from the lagoon where it had crashed. "Size matters not," he tells Luke.

3 ABY: Yoda's humble home on Dagobah is partly constructed from the lifeboat that he travelled to the planet in.

YODA'S HOME

LUKE'S X-WING

3 ABY: Yoda trains Luke's agility and Force abilities.

3 ABY: Luke senses that his friends are in danger and rushes to confront Darth Vader. Yoda and the spirit of Obi-Wan try to persuade him to complete his training first.

4 ABY: Yoda at last becomes one with the Force, peacefully in his home.

Sleens are insect-eating lizards which live in holes in the ground or hollowed-out logs. SLEEN

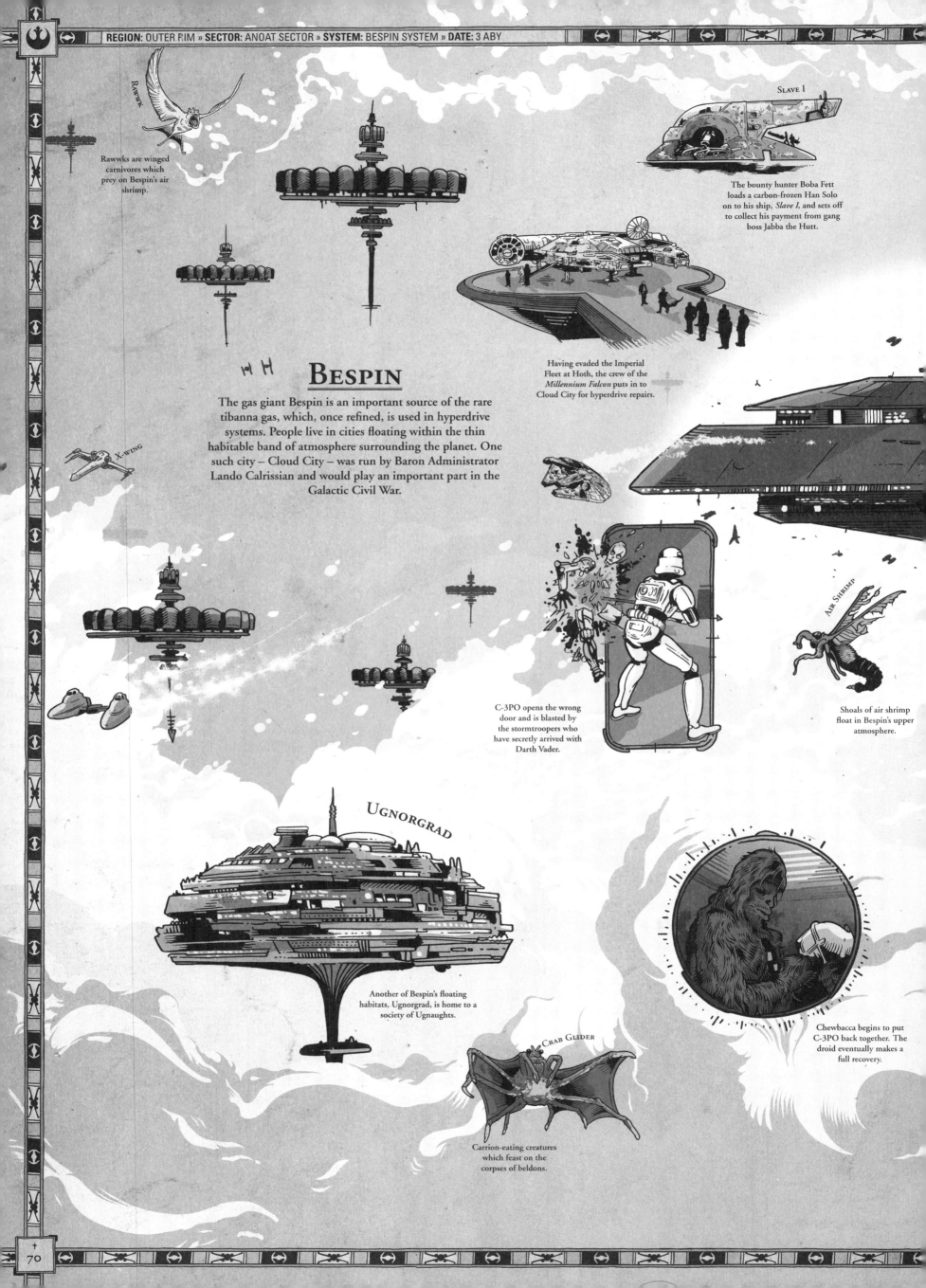

RAWWK

Rawwks are winged carnivores which prey on Bespin's air shrimp.

SLAVE I

The bounty hunter Boba Fett loads a carbon-frozen Han Solo on to his ship, *Slave I*, and sets off to collect his payment from gang boss Jabba the Hutt.

BESPIN

The gas giant Bespin is an important source of the rare tibanna gas, which, once refined, is used in hyperdrive systems. People live in cities floating within the thin habitable band of atmosphere surrounding the planet. One such city – Cloud City – was run by Baron Administrator Lando Calrissian and would play an important part in the Galactic Civil War.

X-WING

Having evaded the Imperial Fleet at Hoth, the crew of the *Millennium Falcon* puts in to Cloud City for hyperdrive repairs.

AIR SHRIMP

C-3PO opens the wrong door and is blasted by the stormtroopers who have secretly arrived with Darth Vader.

Shoals of air shrimp float in Bespin's upper atmosphere.

UGNORGRAD

Another of Bespin's floating habitats, Ugnorgrad, is home to a society of Ugnaughts.

Chewbacca begins to put C-3PO back together. The droid eventually makes a full recovery.

CRAB GLIDER

Carrion-eating creatures which feast on the corpses of beldons.

At the time of the Galactic Civil War, Cloud City is run by Baron Administrator Lando Calrissian, a charismatic ex-smuggler and the former owner of the *Millennium Falcon*.

CLOUD CAR

CLOUD CITY

The city has 392 levels. The top 50 levels are a luxury resort, while the lower levels house gas miners and their machines and equipment.

Boba Fett tracks the *Millennium Falcon* to Cloud City and informs Darth Vader. The Sith Lord sets a trap for Luke Skywalker, using his friends to lure him.

Lando's old comrade Lobot is the computer-liaison officer on Cloud City. His cybernetic implants enable him to interface directly with the city's network.

UGNAUGHT

Ugnaughts do much of the physical labour involved with processing tibanna gas, including the carbon-freezing process that is needed to export it.

When he senses that his friends are in danger, Luke Skywalker abandons his Jedi training and rushes to Cloud City to confront Vader.

The experienced Sith Lord easily defeats the untrained Skywalker, chopping off his right hand. He then reveals that he is Luke's father.

LUKE SKYWALKER

Luke falls from the carbon-freezing chamber, through a shaft, and manages to cling on to an antenna at the bottom of the structure. He calls to Leia using the Force and is rescued.

Luke Skywalker's severed hand and lightsaber fall down the central shaft and are thought lost. Later, however, the lightsaber is recovered.

Vast gas-filled creatures – up to ten kilometres long – which strain nutrients from the atmosphere using their long tentacles.

BELDON

Jedi Master Tu-Anh is murdered on Utapau by Separatist plotters. The Jedi Council send Anakin Skywalker and Obi-Wan Kenobi to investigate.

DACTILLION

Dactillions are giant bird-like creatures that can be used as flying mounts.

UTAPAU

The windswept planet of Utapau is distinctive for its strange terrain, pockmarked with giant sink-holes into which the oceans drain, and its underground cities built from millions of animal bones. It is home to two native species, the Pau'ans and the Utai, as well as more recent arrivals the Amani.

VARACTYL

General Grievous is destroyed by Obi-Wan Kenobi, who tears open his armour and blasts him.

Obi-Wan Kenobi duels General Grievous, but the Kaleesh cyborg escapes and the Jedi gives chase.

Kenobi's troops fire on him and his varactyl mount as Order 66 is issued, but the Jedi escapes.

Anakin Skywalker foils a Separatist plot to obtain a giant kyber crystal, which can be used to create powerful weapons, destroying it instead.

The nos monsters that live in Utapau's lakes can grow up to eight metres long.

Utapau's lakes and rivers drain into the sink-holes, where many strange creatures live.

While investigating Master Tu-Anh's death, Anakin Skywalker discovers Separatist Magna-Guards on the planet.

Recent arrivals on Utapau, the Amani people live in villages on the windswept plains.

Jamels are used by the Amani people to carry heavy loads. They are strong, but slow.

Sugi arms dealers meet with Separatist agents on Utapau to sell a giant kyber crystal. Master Tu-Anh is murdered when she discovers the plot.

The Utai people do much of the manual labour on Utapau, under the direction of their fellow natives the Pau'ans.

General Grievous attempts to escape Obi-Wan Kenobi on his remarkable TSMEU-6 wheel bike.

The Pau'an people live in vast sink-hole cities beneath the planet's surface.

MUSTAFAR

Once described as 'where Jedi go to die', the searing lava-world Mustafar is a world of ill omen. Vast refineries extract precious minerals from the volcanic core of the planet – but it is better known for its history of violence, treachery and death.

LAVA EEL

19 BBY: Obi-Wan Kenobi and Darth Vader duel amid the lava flows. Vader is defeated, and his body mutilated and burned.

3 BBY: Kongo the Disemboweller is employed to keep the dallovite mine tunnels free of xancanks and lava fleas.

19 BBY: Overcome with rage and jealousy, Darth Vader turns on his wife Padmé Amidala and accuses her of betraying him.

21 BBY: Anakin Skywalker and Ahsoka Tano rescue Force-sensitive children from Darth Sidious' secret facility.

Lava fleas skip across the fiery surface of Mustafar. They are large enough to be used as mounts by the native Mustafarians.

Xandanks are insectoid predators native to Mustafar. They hunt in packs and are well protected by armour.

19 bby: Anakin Skywalker, now Darth Vader, slaughters the Separatist leaders at the order of his new Master Darth Sidious. This effectively ends the Clone Wars.

4 bby: The Lothal rebels rescue their comrade Kanan Jarrus from Grand Moff Tarkin's flagship the *Sovereign*, which is destroyed in the process.

4 bby: In a Star Destroyer orbiting Mustafar the Grand Inquisitor is defeated in a duel by the Jedi Kanan Jarrus. Rather than suffer the wrath of Darth Vader, the Inquisitor allows himself to fall to his death.

19 bby: Mustafar was once home to the Black Sun crime syndicate. Their leader Xomit Grunseit, a Falleen, was killed when Darth Maul took over the organisation.

BESTIARY

Showing the relative sizes of the various
strange creatures in these maps.

NOS MONSTER

MON CALA EEL

KWAZEL MAW

DEWBACK

SWAMP SLUG

WAMPA

WOOLAMANDER

LOTH-CAT

KAADU

MARSH SPIDER

RANCOR

TUSK-CAT

BLURRG

RONTO

BANTHA

LYLEK

EOPIE

STINTARIL

GUTKURR

XANDANK

JUBBA BIRD

RAWWK

CAN-CELL

GORSIAN DRAGONFLY

AIWHA

GORSIAN DRAGONFLY

WHISPER BIRD

DACTILLION

BELDON TENTACLES

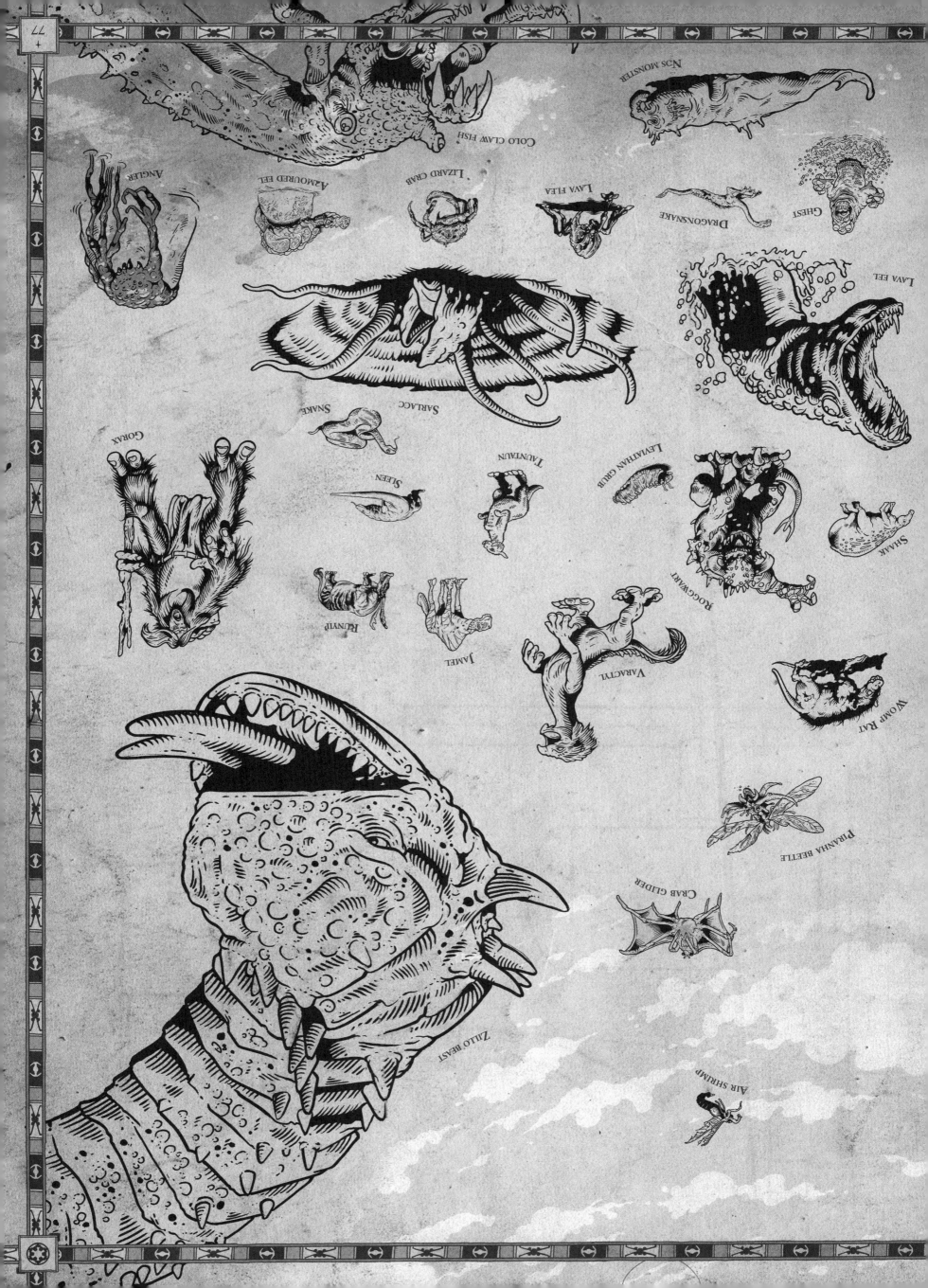